continued on next page . . .

"Parker's debut thriller featuring Jesse Stone will leave you looking forward to the second installment."
—*Atlanta Journal-Constitution*

"Not for nothing is Parker regarded as the reigning champion of the American tough-guy detective novel, heavyweight division. Over a twenty-five-year career, the man has rarely composed a bad sentence or an inert paragraph. His thirtieth novel, which features brand-new protagonist Jesse Stone . . . proves no exception."
—*Entertainment Weekly*

"Move over, Spenser. A new hero has moved into your neighborhood. And for that, you can thank your own creator—Robert B. Parker . . . His writing—tough, witty, lean, with a touch of the poet—has never been better."
—*Lexington Herald-Leader*

"Moments of real wit and depth."
—*The Seattle Times & Post-Intelligencer*

"Stone is an intriguing character . . . the dialogue sparkles."
—*San Antonio Express-News*

"Exceedingly satisfying."
—*Publishers Weekly*

"Parker, with his usual great dialogue and story line, has given us another tough hero."
—*Sunday Oklahoman*

"An attractive protagonist."
—*San Diego Union-Tribune*

"A first-rate, engrossing book."
—*Florida Times-Union*

"A new series that's already off to a good start."
—*Orlando Sentinel*

continued on next page . . .

Double Deuce

Spenser and Hawk wage war on a street gang . . . "MR. SPENSER IS AT HIS BEST . . . TENSE . . . SUSPENSEFUL . . . DARKLY POETIC." —*The New York Times*

Pastime

A boy's search for his mother forces Spenser to face his own past . . . "EMOTIONALLY TENSE . . . GRIPPING . . . VINTAGE HARD-CORE SPENSER." —*Kirkus Reviews*

Stardust

Spenser tries to protect a TV star from a would-be assassin . . . "CLASSIC SPENSER . . . BRILLIANT."
—*The New York Times Book Review*

Playmates

Spenser scores against corruption in the world of college basketball . . . "A WHOLE LOTTA FUN . . . KICK BACK AND ENJOY." —*New York Daily News*

Perchance to Dream

Robert B. Parker's acclaimed sequel to the Raymond Chandler classic *The Big Sleep,* featuring detective Philip Marlowe . . . "A STUNNING, DROP-DEAD SUCCESS . . . DAZZLING." —*Publishers Weekly*

Poodle Springs

Raymond Chandler's unfinished Marlowe thriller—completed by today's master of detective fiction, Robert B. Parker . . . "A FIRST-RATE DETECTIVE NOVEL WITH ALL THE SUSPENSE, ACTION, AND HUMAN DRAMA THAT WE HAVE COME TO EXPECT FROM THE BEST." —*Playboy*

Trouble in Paradise

Robert B. Parker

BERKLEY BOOKS, NEW YORK

THE BERKLEY PUBLISHING GROUP
Published by the Penguin Group
Penguin Group (USA) Inc.
375 Hudson Street, New York, New York 10014, USA
Penguin Group (Canada), 90 Eglinton Avenue East, Suite 700, Toronto, Ontario M4P 2Y3, Canada
(a division of Pearson Penguin Canada Inc.)
Penguin Books Ltd., 80 Strand, London WC2R 0RL, England
Penguin Group Ireland, 25 St. Stephen's Green, Dublin 2, Ireland (a division of Penguin Books Ltd.)
Penguin Group (Australia), 250 Camberwell Road, Camberwell, Victoria 3124, Australia
(a division of Pearson Australia Group Pty. Ltd.)
Penguin Books India Pvt. Ltd., 11 Community Centre, Panchsheel Park, New Delhi—110 017, India
Penguin Group (NZ), 67 Apollo Drive, Rosedale, North Shore 0745, Auckland, New Zealand
(a division of Pearson New Zealand Ltd.)
Penguin Books (South Africa) (Pty.) Ltd., 24 Sturdee Avenue, Rosebank, Johannesburg 2196,
South Africa

Penguin Books Ltd., Registered Offices: 80 Strand, London WC2R 0RL, England

TROUBLE IN PARADISE

A Berkley Book / published by arrangement with the author

PRINTING HISTORY
G. P. Putnam's Sons edition / September 1998
Jove mass-market edition / October 1999
Berkley mass-market edition / August 2007

ISBN: 978-0-425-22110-5

BERKLEY®
Berkley Books are published by The Berkley Publishing Group,
a division of Penguin Group (USA) Inc.,
375 Hudson Street, New York, New York 10014.
BERKLEY® is a registered trademark of Penguin Group (USA) Inc.
The "B" design is a trademark belonging to Penguin Group (USA) Inc.

PRINTED IN THE UNITED STATES OF AMERICA

25   24   23   22   21   20   19   18   17

FOR JOAN:
Paradise Regained

Trouble in Paradise

chapter 1

When he was sleepless, which was less often than it used
to be, Jesse Stone would get into the black Explorer he'd
driven from L.A. and cruise around Paradise, Massachusetts, where he was chief of police. Nights like tonight,
with the rain slanting down through the dark, and the
streets shiny in the headlights, were the ones Jesse liked
best. It would have been nice, Jesse thought, on a night
like this, to have been a town marshal somewhere in the
old west, where he could have relaxed into the saddle
under his oilskin slicker with his hat yanked down over his
eyes and let the horse find its own direction. He drove
slowly past the town common with its white colonial
meetinghouse on which the rain had fallen for two hundred years. The blue glare of the mercury street lamps dif-
fused by the rain was restrained and opalescent. Except for
the headlights of the Explorer, there were no other lights
in this part of town. The neat houses with large lawns
around the common were still and unlit. Nothing moved.
The town library was blank. The high school stood inert,

its red brick glistening with rain, its black windows
implacable in the arc of headlights as Jesse turned into the
parking lot.

He stopped the car for a moment and flicked on the high
beams. The headlights rested on the baseball diamond: the
rusting screen of the backstop, the slab of rubber on the
pitcher's mound, bowed slightly, the hollow in front of it
where the high school kids lunged off the rubber, trying to
pitch off leg drive like Nolan Ryan. When he'd been in the
minors, he could play the deepest short in the league
because he had the big arm and could make the throw
from the hole. Gave him range. Gave him more time. He
could run. He had good hands. He could hit enough for a
middle infielder. But it was the arm. Bigger arm than Rick
Burleson, they used to tell him. Ticket to the show. Jesse
rubbed his right shoulder as he looked at the baseball field.
He remembered when he hurt it, at the start of a double
play. It had been a clean take out. And it ended his
career. . . .

Jesse let the car slide forward and turned and went
down Main Street toward the water. He pulled off the
street into the empty parking lot at Paradise Beach. He
let the motor idle. The rain intensified the sea smell. In
the headlights the surf came in and curled and crested
and broke, the black ocean making the hard rain seem
trivial. A thermos of piña coladas would be nice to
drink sitting here, and maybe some music. He thought
about Jenn. She had an infinite capacity for romance. If
she were here, she would lean back with her eyes closed
and talk with him and listen to him and let herself feel
the romance of the late night and the rain and the sound
of the ocean. And let him share it with her. Sometimes
he thought he missed that more than anything else in
the marriage. Ten years in L.A. Homicide hadn't
extinguished his sense of romantic possibility. It had
demonstrated beyond argument that romance was not
at all likely. But in showing its evanescence, experience
had made Jesse more certain that the possibility of

romance was the final stay against confusion. Maybe
for Jenn too. Long after the divorce, they were still
connected. When she heard last year that he was in trouble, she'd come east. It wasn't the kind of trouble she
could help with. She would have known that. She had
come, simply, he supposed, when he allowed himself
to think about it, to be there. And she was still here,
living here. And what the hell were they going to do
now? He put the car in drive and turned slowly out of
the parking lot and drove along the beachfront toward
downtown. Neither booze nor his ex-wife were good for
him, and he shouldn't spend too much time thinking of
them.

The marquee of the movie theater was unlit. The stores
were dark. The street lights cycled through the red, yellow, green changes unobserved. He went up Indian Hill
and into Hawthorne Park. He parked very near the edge of
the high ground and shut off the headlights and let the car
idle again while he looked out over the harbor. To his left
the harbor emptied into the open ocean. To his right the
harbor dead-ended at the causeway that ran from Paradise
to Paradise Neck. The neck was straight across the harbor,
a low dark form with a lighthouse on the north point. Just
inside the lighthouse point, a hundred yards off shore,
crossing the T of the point at a slant, was Stiles Island. The
near end of it shielded the harbor mouth, the far end jutted
beyond the point into the open sea. In the channel,
between the island and the neck, where the land pressed
the water on either side, Jesse knew that the ocean currents
seethed dangerously, and the water was never still. But
from here, there was no hint of it. The calm sweep of the
lighthouse just touched the expensive rooftops of the carefully spaced houses, and ran the full length of the barrel-
arched bridge that connected it to the neck. The rest was
darkness.

Jesse sat for a long time in the darkness looking at the
ocean and the rain. The digital clock on the dash read 4:23.
In clear weather the eastern sky would be pale by now and

in another half hour or so, this time of year, it would be light. Jesse turned on the headlights and backed the car up and headed back down the hill to shower and change and put on his badge.

chapter 2

By the time Macklin was out of jail for a week, he had acquired a brown Mercedes sedan, which he stole from the Alewife Station parking garage, and a 9-mm semiautomatic pistol that he got from a guy he'd done time with named Desmond. Macklin used the nine to knock over a liquor store near Wellington Circle. With the money from the liquor store, he paid Desmond's cousin Chick, who worked at the Registry of Motor Vehicles, to fix up a registration in the name of Harry Smith and scam a legitimate license plate. He had the car painted British racing green. Then he bought a fifth of Belvedere vodka and a bottle of Stock vermouth and drove over to see Faye.

As soon as he walked in the apartment, she slipped out of the bathrobe she was wearing and in five minutes they were making love. When it was over, Faye got up and made them each a martini and brought the drinks back to bed.

"Saved that up for a year and a half," Macklin said.

"I could tell," Faye said.

They were propped among the pink and lavender pillows on Faye's king-sized bed with the martinis next to Macklin's pistol on the bedside table. The bedroom walls were lavender, and the ceiling was mirrored. The condominium was in the old Charlestown Navy Yard, and through the second floor windows they could see the Boston skyline across the harbor.

"You too?" Macklin said.

"Me too what?" Faye said.

She had a rose tattooed at the top of her right thigh.

"You been saving it for a year and a half?"

"Of course," she said.

Macklin drank some of his martini. The sheets on Faye's bed were lavender.

"Nobody else?"

"Nobody," Faye said.

Staring up at the mirrored ceiling, she liked the way they looked. He was slim and smooth. He was so blond that his hair was nearly white. He looked a little pale now, but she knew he'd get his tan back. She loved the contrast of his white-blond hair and his tan skin. She examined herself carefully. Boobs still good. Legs still good. They ought to be. Forty-five minutes every day on the goddamned StairMaster. She rolled onto her side, and looked at her butt. Tight. StairMaster does it again.

"Checking out the equipment?" Macklin said.

"Uh-huh."

"Seems to be working okay," Macklin said.

She giggled.

"How about yours?" she said.

"Pretty soon."

They finished their martinis in silence.

"What are we going to do?" Faye said.

"The same thing mostly," Macklin said, "but I was thinking maybe we could try it in the chair."

Faye giggled again. "I don't mean that," she said. "I mean what are we going to do, you know, like with our life?"

"Besides this?"

"Besides this."

Macklin smiled. He sat up higher in the bed and poured another martini for himself and one for Faye.

"Well, tomorrow," Macklin said, "we're going up to Paradise and look at real estate on Stiles Island."

"What's Stiles Island?"

"Island in Paradise Harbor. It's connected to the rest of the town by a little bridge. Bridge is gated and there's a guard shack and a private security patrol. Everybody lives there is rich. They got a branch bank out there just for them."

"How do you know about this place?"

"Guy I was in jail with, Lester Lang, kept talking about it, called it the mother lode."

"You ever seen it?"

"Nope."

"We going to buy property out there?" Faye said.

"Nope."

"So why we going up there to look at real estate?"

"We're scoping the place."

"For what?"

"For the mother of all stickups," Macklin said.

Faye put her head against his shoulder and laughed. "I'll drink to that," she said, touching the rim of her glass to the rim of his.

chapter 3

Suitcase Simpson came through the open door into Jesse's office without knocking. He said, "Jesse, was that your ex-wife I seen on TV last night?"

"I don't know, Suit," Jesse said. "What did you see?"

"Channel Three News," Simpson said. "They got a new weather girl, Jenn Stone."

She'd used her married name.

"Weather girl?" Jesse said.

"Yeah, they said she was from Los Angeles and were joking around with her about how it would be pretty different trying to report New England weather."

"And it looked like Jenn?"

"Yeah, I only seen her that one time, but you know she's not somebody you forget."

"No," Jesse said, "she's not."

"Was she a weather girl in L.A.?" Simpson said.

"No, she was an actress."

"Well, maybe she's acting like a weather girl."

"Maybe," Jesse said. "Was she on at six or eleven?"

"I saw her at six," Simpson said.

"I'll take a look tonight," Jesse said.

"I guess she's not going back to L.A.," Simpson said.

"Looks that way for now," Jesse said.

Simpson stood for a moment, as if he wanted to say other things but didn't know how to. Finally he said, "Well, I figured you'd want to know."

"I would, thanks, Suit."

Simpson hesitated another moment and then nodded as if answering yes to a question no one had asked, turned, and went out of the office.

She's using her married name.

Jesse swiveled his chair around and put his feet up on the windowsill and looked out. It has to be Jenn, he thought. It's too big a coincidence. Three thousand miles away from her, he'd gotten his feelings under control. He hadn't stopped loving her, but the fact that he did love her didn't mean he had to be with her, and it didn't mean he couldn't love anybody else. Or at least it hadn't meant that, or he'd thought it hadn't meant that, while she was three thousand miles away in bed with a movie producer. But here . . .

Molly Crane came in from the desk.

"Jesse," she said, "the fire this morning down at Fifty-nine Geary Street? Anthony says it looks like it was set, thinks you should have a look."

Jesse swiveled slowly back around.

"Geary Street," he said.

"They got the fire pretty well knocked down," Molly said. "But Anthony's there and the fire captain."

Jesse nodded.

"They're waiting on you, Jesse."

Jesse smiled. Molly was like a third-grade teacher.

"On my way," he said.

He didn't use the siren. One of his hard rules for the department was no sirens, no flashing lights, unless it was a time-sensitive emergency.

That end of Geary Street converged with Preston Road to form a triangle two blocks from the beach. Fifty-nine

Geary was at the apex of the triangle. It was separated from the next house by a vacant lot. Both Geary and Preston were blocked off when Jesse arrived. Pat Sears was rerouting traffic away from the area. Jesse stopped beside him.

"You want me to get couple more people down here for traffic?" he said.

Pat blew his whistle and vigorously gestured a Buick station wagon to proceed past Jesse's car.

"You bet," he said to Jesse. "We need somebody down the other end, and maybe another guy up there." He nodded toward the traffic trying to inch past the fire captain's car that jutted out into LaSalle Street.

"I'll call Molly," Jesse said and drove down to the fire scene.

There were half a dozen fire trucks. Both of the Paradise trucks and four from neighboring departments. Jesse parked among them and got out. Arleigh Baker, the fire captain, was standing on the front lawn. Technically, as director of Public Safety, Jesse was the fire chief too. But since Jesse knew little about fighting fires, and Arleigh knew a lot, Arleigh ran the fire department. He was short and fat and looked slightly Napoleonic in his helmet, boots, and raincoat.

"Looking good, Arleigh," Jesse said.

"I look like a goddamned asshole in this outfit," Arleigh said.

Jesse smiled, and looked at the still smoking remnant of the house. Its superstructure was still standing. There was a hole in the roof, and all the windows were out. Part of the front wall had burned away. Inside was black with ash and crisscrossed with charred timber.

"Suspicious origin?" Jesse said.

"Take a look," Arleigh said and started for the front door.

The fire had been at its most intense in the living room, to the right as Jesse entered the front door. Most of the floor was gone, and part of the back wall had burned through to the kitchen behind it. On the left-hand wall, where the fire hadn't bitten, the word FAGGOTS was spray painted in large black letters.

"Watch your step," Arleigh said.

Jesse was wearing sneakers. The floor was still warm in places and there were pieces of lath lying about bristling with thin-shanked nails. Jesse stepped carefully through the debris. In his boots, Arleigh paid it no heed.

Up the stairwell it said FAGGOTS, and in two of the upstairs rooms, where the damage was largely smoke staining, the word was curlicued repetitively on the walls.

"Not an inventive bastard," Jesse said.

"We'll have the state fire marshal in here later on," Arleigh said. "Give us something more definitive. But it looks to me that the fire started right in the middle of the living room floor. That's unusual, unless somebody just dumped a can of gasoline on the rug and let her rip."

He was red-faced and sweating inside his heavy coat.

"And if it was set, it's logical to assume that the people who wrote FAGGOTS did the setting."

"People? Plural?"

"Yeah," Jesse said. "At least two people did the graffiti."

"How the hell can you tell?" Arleigh said.

"Work South Central L.A. for a while," Jesse said, "get to see a lot of taggers. You know who lives here?"

"No."

"We'll ask around," Jesse said.

chapter 4

"This is not encouraging," Macklin said as he slowed the Mercedes. The traffic was at a dead stop ahead on LaSalle Street. "We want to take that right."

"There's a cop directing traffic," Faye said. "He's not letting anyone down there."

"Fire," Macklin said. "See the fire chief car sticking out into the road? That's what's causing the whole thing." He shook his head. "Firemen and cops," he said. "Park any friggin' place they feel like it. Don't give a goddamn how bad they screw up the traffic."

Macklin had spent time in the tanning salon at Faye's complex so he had a prosperous tan. He was wearing a gray Palm Beach suit and a blue oxford shirt with a button-down collar. He had on a yellow silk tie and a yellow pocket silk. The 9-mm pistol was in the glove compartment.

"How hard would it have been," he said, "for the ass-hole to have pulled up onto the grass?"

Faye smiled. She had on a subdued tan suit, with a long jacket and short skirt, and her hair was up and gathered in a French twist at the back. The car inched forward.

"It's a house fire," Faye said. "I can see the trucks down the side street."

"And they can't fight it without fucking up the traffic all the way back to Lynn?" Macklin said.

"I think it's out," Faye said.

"It's like the law don't apply to them, you know? Like there's one law for us and no law at all for them," Macklin said.

Faye turned and looked at him. She smiled widely.

"There's a law for us?" she said. "Jimmy, you're a crook. You don't pay any attention to the law at all."

Macklin inched past the cop directing traffic and squeezed past the fire captain's car and picked up speed. His shoulders were shaking with silent laughter.

"Oh yeah," he said.

They turned right past the movie theater and drove along Ocean Avenue to Preston Road past Geary Street, which was still closed off, to the causeway and out onto Paradise Neck. The neck was thick with trees and big lawns, the big old shingle houses back from the narrow road and barely visible. They went past the yacht club, a rambling white building that faced the harbor, and around lighthouse point and pulled onto the elegant little bridge that arched the narrow stretch of angry surf to Stiles Island. On the island end was a guard shack. Macklin stopped and lowered his window. A tallish, gray-haired man in glasses came out wearing a blue blazer and carrying a clipboard. A blue plastic name tag on his blazer said STILES ISLAND SECURITY and under that his name, J. T. McGonigle.

"Hi," Macklin said, "we have an appointment with Mrs. Campbell."

"Your name, sir?"

"I know this sounds corny," Macklin said, "but it's Smith."

The guard consulted his clipboard. "Mr. and Mrs.?"

"Yep."

"Right over there, sir. Please park in the designated space."

"Thank you."

As they drove through the gate, the guard copied down the license plate number. Past the guard shack, to the right, was a small building done in weathered shingles with colonial blue shutters. A discreet sign beside the door said STILES ISLAND REALTY in gold letters on a dark blue background. A Lexus sedan was parked next to the building, and two spaces beside it were marked VISITORS.

"Stiles Island is too classy to have customers," Macklin said.

"What are our first names?" Faye said.

"I'll be Harry," Macklin said. "You got a favorite?"

"How about one of those really jerky names that WASP women have, like Muffy or Choo Choo?"

"Jesus," Macklin said, "I can't go around calling you fucking Muffy."

"Rocky?" Faye said.

"Rocky?" Macklin said.

Faye nodded. Macklin nodded and put out his clenched fist. Faye tapped it lightly with hers.

"Way to go, Rocky," he said.

They got out of the car.

"Where we from?" Faye said.

"I'll think of someplace," Macklin said. "You know how I hate to plan stuff."

The real estate office was furnished with colonial furniture and nautical prints. Mrs. Campbell was a tall woman with platinum hair, a lot of makeup, and a good figure. She was a little long in the tooth, Macklin thought, but she'd probably be a pretty good lay.

"I'm Harry Smith," Macklin said. "My wife, Rocky."

"Where you folks from?" Mrs. Campbell said.

She was wearing a blue pantsuit and a white man-tailored shirt, open at the throat.

"Concord," Macklin said.

"And you're interested in property on Stiles Island?"

"Yes, ma'am," Macklin said.

"Well, we have a couple of homes for sale, and of course, we can arrange for you to build if you wish."

"What do you think, hon?" Macklin said.

"I think the first thing we should do is tour the island," Faye said. "We're not just purchasing a piece of property, you know. We are buying into a community."

"Good point," Mrs. Campbell said. "Why don't I drive you around and acquaint you with the place, and we can talk as we go. Will you be financing this purchase yourself?"

"It'll be cash," Macklin said.

"And are you more interested in building or buying something already built?"

"We're open on that," Faye said. "Aren't we, Harry?"

"Sure are, Rocky."

Mrs. Campbell went around her desk to get her purse. Macklin noticed that the pantsuit fit snugly over her butt. And there was something in the way she walked. Fucks like a weasel, Macklin thought. He didn't know exactly how he knew that. Maybe the way she stood or the way she walked or the sense of how conscious she was of her body. Maybe it was magic. But he was rarely wrong about such things. He filed the information.

chapter 5

The two men who owned the home on Geary Street sat together in Jesse's office. One was a tall slim man with a shaved head and a dark tan. He wore gold-rimmed aviator sunglasses. His companion was stockier, with a blond crew cut and a clipped moustache. Both men were older than Jesse. Forty-two, forty-three, Jesse speculated. The taller man's name was Alex Canton.

"We were in Provincetown for a few days when it happened," Canton said. "One of the neighbors called us. We came right back."

"The fire was set," Jesse said. "We assumed it was because of the graffiti, and the way the floor burned. But the state Fire Marshal's Office makes it definite. A combustible liquid, probably gasoline, was poured over the rug in the living room and ignited."

"We know who did it," Canton said. "Howard and I are both sure of it."

Jesse glanced at the notes on his yellow legal pad. Howard's last name was Brown.

"Who?" Jesse said.

"Alex, we can't really prove it," Brown said.

"We know it was them," Canton said.

"Who?" Jesse said.

"The fucking Hopkins kids," Canton said.

"Full names?"

"Earl," Canton said, "I think is the older one. And Robbie."

"Ages?"

"Oh, maybe fifteen and fourteen, in there. Neither one of them drives a car yet."

"Had trouble with them before?" Jesse said.

He knew the answer before he asked the question. Of course they'd had trouble. Two openly gay men in an openly heterosexual environment with a lot of affluent teenage kids hanging around with nothing to do. Let's go down and harass the queers.

"Nothing big, they'd make remarks when they went by the house," Brown said.

"Such as?"

"Oh, some kind of rhyme about Mister Brown goes down. Stuff like that. I been gay a long time. I've heard worse."

"Anything else?"

Brown and Canton looked at each other as they thought about it.

"No," Canton said.

"Mr. Brown?"

"No, uh-uh."

"So how do you know they set the fire?"

Canton looked at Brown. "You say, Howard."

"I was standing in the driveway, looking at what's left, and they came riding by on bicycles. Both the Hopkins boys and their friend. I don't know his real name, kids call him Snapper. They all had these big smirks on, and they sort of slow down and start riding their bicycles in big circles in the street. Then the older one, Earl, starts riding no hands and he says to me, 'Hey Mr. Brown,' and I looked, and he made a gesture of lighting and throwing a match. And all three of them are smirking."

Brown shook his head. "I wanted to kill the little punks."

He shook his head again. Sadness and anger about equal, Jesse thought.

"But of course, I didn't say a word. I just got in my car and drove off," Brown said.

"They ever threaten you?" Jesse said.

"Not until this," Canton said.

Brown shook his head.

"Well, we'll talk with them," Jesse said.

"Talk. The little bastards burned our house down and you'll talk with them?"

"It's a cop euphemism," Jesse said. "I'll have them in. We'll question them."

"You can't arrest them?" Brown said.

"Not on what you've given me."

"They practically admitted they did it," Brown said.

"Or maybe they just took pleasure in reminding you someone did it," Jesse said.

"If you'd been there and seen the look on their faces, all three of them," Brown said.

"But I wasn't," Jesse said. "And the DA wasn't. I can't get them indicted on what you've said."

"So they'll get away with it," Canton said, like a man confirming a long-held assumption.

"Maybe not," Jesse said. "We're kind of resourceful."

"Well," Canton said. "I tell you one thing right now. I'm getting a gun. I'm not going to let the yahoos win."

"See Molly at the desk," Jesse said. "She processes the gun stuff."

"You'll approve it?"

"You have the constitutional right to keep and bear arms," Jesse said.

"Christ," Canton said, "I never thought I'd need to."

"Hopkins family got money?" Jesse said.

"I think so," Brown said. "Why?"

"Turns out the kid did it, you might have a civil suit against the family, or your insurance company might."

"My God, I never thought of it," Canton said. "Should we talk to our claims adjuster about it?"

"Might be wise to talk first with a lawyer," Jesse said.

"You recommend anyone?"

"There's a woman in town," Jesse said. "Abby Taylor. Used to be town counsel. She can either help you or send you to somebody."

"But what if you can't prove they did it?" Canton said.

"You can still sue," Jesse said. "Civil cases have different rules."

"Could you write that lawyer's name down?" Brown said.

Jesse wrote Abby's name on a sheet of yellow paper, along with her phone number, which he knew quite well. Brown took the paper and folded it over and slipped it into his shirt pocket.

"So that's going to be it?" Canton said.

"Is what going to be it?" Jesse said.

"That's your little law enforcement gesture? Give us the name of a lawyer, tell us to sue?"

Jesse leaned back in his chair and looked at Canton for a moment.

"You're a gay man," Jesse said. "And you're mad as hell. And you're not used to straight cops working very hard to solve your problems. But maybe you should wait until I take a run at the thing, before you decide I'm an incompetent bigot."

"That's fair enough," Brown said. "We can't assume he's a homophobe, Alex."

"Maybe," Canton said. "But he's one of the few I've met that aren't."

He stared hard at Jesse, a red flush of anger still brightening his face.

"I'm not so sure," Jesse said. "There might be a lot of cops who don't really much care what you do with a consenting adult."

"You've never been gay," Canton said.

"You have me there," Jesse said. "And you didn't come here to argue police tolerance with me. What I can do is tell you that everyone in this town is entitled to the protection of the police. And everyone will get it as long as I'm chief. Including you."

"Alex, he has the right to prove his homophobia before we condemn him."

"And he probably will," Canton said. "I'm going to apply for that gun permit. Don't think I won't."

Jesse smiled pleasantly.

"I don't think you won't," he said.

chapter 6

Macklin sat with Faye on the deck outside the Gray Gull Restaurant overlooking the harbor. They were drinking cosmopolitans. Faye had hers straight up in a big martini glass. Macklin was drinking his on the rocks. The late afternoon sun had gotten low enough behind the buildings to throw elongated shadows of the wharf office and the sail loft out onto the water.

"Faye," Macklin said, "you look more like the wife of a WASP millionaire than any of the real ones I've ever known."

"So maybe that means I don't," Faye said. "And exactly how many WASP millionaires' wives have you known?"

"If I knew one, she'd look like you," Macklin said.

He had loosened his tie and taken off his coat. He sat now with his legs out in front of him, leaning back in his chair. There was a breeze off the water.

"You told that woman we were from Concord," Faye said.

"Sure," Macklin said. "I lived there for a couple years."

"In Concord?"

Macklin grinned. "MCI Concord," he said. "The prison."

Faye laughed. "Jimmy, you're crazy."

"Can't get too solemn about this shit," Macklin said.

A waitress went by. Macklin gestured at her for a refill.

"And maybe, whaddya got. Some fried clams? Give us an order of fried clams," he said. "But bring the drinks first. Don't wait for the clams."

"Yes sir."

Macklin watched her as she walked away. Nice butt. Young. Probably some college kid working for the summer.

"So what did we learn about Stiles Island today?" Faye said.

"Three quarters of a mile long," Macklin said, gazing out across the harbor at the near end of it. "About a quarter of a mile wide. Fifty estates so far. Room to build another fifty. Cheapest one is eight hundred seventy-five thousand dollars. Adults only. No children. No dogs."

"Most people can afford eight-hundred-seventy-five-thousand-dollar houses are too old to have children anyway," Faye said.

Macklin nodded.

"Only access is across that bridge," he said. "All the power lines are under the bridge, all the phone lines, even the water pipes are incorporated into the bridge understructure."

The waitress brought them two more cosmopolitans. The pink drinks looked just right, Macklin thought, out here on the deck of the weathered shingle restaurant with the harbor below them. Macklin liked things to be right.

"There's a branch of Paradise Bank," he said. "With safe deposit boxes. There's a private boat club on the harbor end of the island, only place on the island where you can land a boat. There's a health club with a drug store and beauty salon and a restaurant with a big plate glass picture window looking out on the ocean side. And there's a private security patrol, a man on the bridge twenty-four hours, and a two-man cruiser patrolling the island twenty-four hours. Everybody got a radio that connects to the security headquarters in the other side of the real estate office and to the Paradise Police."

Faye held her glass with the fingertips of both hands. She was watching him over the rim of it as he talked. When he finished she whistled very softly. "And I thought all you were doing was watching Mrs. Campbell's ass," she said.

Macklin grinned. "Attention to detail," he said.

A gull coasted down, sat on the fence railing about five feet away, and waited. The waitress brought flatware wrapped in napkins, and an order of fried clams in a small paper napkin–lined wicker basket. She put the clams on the table between them and placed two small paper cups of tartar sauce beside the basket.

"Catsup?" she said.

"No, thank you very much," Macklin said.

The gull fixed its opaque stare on the clams. Macklin unwrapped his flatware and tucked the napkin in under his chin. He picked up the knife and made a fencer's pose at the gull.

"One move at the clams, bird, and you die," Macklin said.

Faye picked up a clam with her fingers, dabbed it in the tartar sauce, and popped it in her mouth. She wiped her fingertips carefully with her napkin while she chewed her clam.

When she swallowed it, she said, "So what is your plan?"

"Well," Macklin said, "I thought I might give Mrs. Campbell a ringy dingy . . ."

"Like hell," Faye said. "Looking is one thing. You're a man, and you can't help it. But you start following up, and I will cut off your balls."

"Faye, would I cheat on you?"

"Like I say, you're a man."

"Cynical," Macklin said.

"Experienced," Faye said. "Besides, you know what I

meant. What is your plan for doing business on the island?"

"Well I'm going to get a good map," Macklin said. "And I'm going to start putting together a crew."

"What are we going to do for money in the meantime?"

"I'll get some," Macklin said.

"I hope so. You got people in mind for this crew?"

"Yeah. It's one of the best things about going to jail a few times," Macklin said. "You get a chance to network."

"You going to hit the bank?"

"Sweet cakes," Macklin said, "I'm going to hit the whole island."

chapter 7

As he had taken to doing when his day ended at five, Jesse stopped by the bar at the Gray Gull. He would have two drinks, talk with the bartender or a few of the regulars, and then go home for supper. It worked better than having a drink at home. It was sociable, and it was easier to stop after two in public. Being chief of police carried with it certain obligations, and Jesse was pretty sure that not getting drunk in public was one of them.

"Black label and soda, Doc," Jesse said to the bartender. He made a measuring gesture with his hands. "Tall glass."

The bartender made the drink and set it before Jesse and went down to the service corner of the bar to get a waitress order. He mixed up two pink drinks, one of them up, the other on the rocks, and set them out with the slip tucked between the glasses. Then he came back down the bar to talk with Jesse.

"You been fighting crime all day?" Doc said.

"Serve and protect," Jesse said. "What are those pink things?"

"Cosmopolitans," Doc said. "Sort of a summer martini."

"They look tasty," Jesse said.

"They're pretty good," Doc said. "You want to try one? On me?"

The young waitress came and put the two drinks on a tray and went out onto the deck with them. Jesse noticed that her cutoff jeans were snug.

"No thanks, Doc. Scotch is fine."

Jesse nursed his drink. The bar was only half full. It was midweek, and the after-work crowd hadn't drifted in yet in force. Jesse liked quiet bars. He liked them best in the middle of the afternoon, air-conditioned and nearly empty, where everything was desultory and you could play old Carl Perkins stuff on the juke box and watch people as they came in out of the outside brightness and paused for their eyes to adjust. He liked the lucent way the bottles looked, arranged along the back of a good bar with the mirror reflecting the light from behind them. It was a little too late to be perfect, but it was still a good place to be. For two drinks.

In the bar mirror, he saw Abby Taylor come into the bar with a tall man in a seersucker suit. Jesse smiled. Only here, Jesse thought. Until a year ago, he'd never seen a seersucker suit. They got a table behind him and sat. Abby saw him then and said something to the man and got up and walked over. She was wearing an olive suit with a short skirt.

"Jesse," she said. "How are you?"

They shook hands, and she put her cheek out. Jesse kissed it lightly.

"Fine," Jesse said. "You look great."

Behind her Jesse could see the guy in the seersucker suit order drinks from a waitress. He was nearly bald, with what remained of his hair cut short.

"Thanks, you too. How are you and Jenn getting on?"

Jesse shrugged. "She came back because I was in trouble. Now I'm not in trouble. She hasn't been around much. Suit tells me he saw her doing the weather on Channel Three."

"So you're not together?"

"God no," Jesse said.

"But you're not fully apart," Abby said. "Are you?"

"I guess not," Jesse said. "That the new boyfriend?"

"Chip? Maybe. We've been dating for a while."

"Chip?" Jesse said.

"I know, but he's really nice. He knows about us. Want to meet him?"

"No," Jesse said.

The young waitress with the tight cutoffs came out of the kitchen with a basket of clams and walked past them toward the deck. Jesse watched her. Abby smiled.

"Good to see you've not lost all interest," Abby said.

"I don't think that's possible," Jesse said.

"Well . . ." Abby paused a moment, thinking of what to say. "I hope you and Jenn work it out, whatever way is best for you."

"When we got divorced I thought we had," Jesse said.

"One would have thought that," Abby said and patted his hand lightly where it rested on the bar. "Take care of yourself."

"You too," Jesse said.

He watched her as she walked back to sit down with Chip. Chip looked over at him and nodded in a friendly way. Fuck you, Chip.

"Better hit me again, Doc," Jesse said.

The second drink tasted better than the first. Jesse held it up so that the light shown through it. The ice cubes were crystalline. The drink was golden with scotch and quick with carbonation.

"You know a family in town named Hopkins?"

"Yeah. He's some kind of financial consultant, I think."

"Kids?"

"They got a couple," Doc said. "Kids are real assholes."

"Lot of that going around," Jesse said.

"Yeah, all fifteen-year-old kids are probably assholes," Doc said. "But these kids are worse. You know I got a lobster boat."

Jesse nodded.

"I caught them one day stealing lobsters out of my boat while I was in the wharf office for a minute."

"Maybe they were having a clam bake," Jesse said.

"They weren't taking them. They weren't even throwing them back. They were stealing them and throwing them up onto the deck of some guy's Chris-Craft."

"So the lobsters die and the guy's boat gets messed up and you lose money and all they get out of it is the pleasure of being pricks," Jesse said.

"Jesse, you're wasting your time as a cop. You should be a child psychologist," Doc said. "I wanted to drown the little fuckers."

"But you didn't."

Doc shrugged. The sleeves of his white shirt were rolled above his elbows and his sun-darkened forearms were those of a man who'd done a lot of heavy physical labor in his life.

"They're too old to scare, too young to kick the shit out of. I chased them off, climbed on the Chris-Craft, and got my lobsters back."

"Say anything to the parents?"

"No."

Doc moved down the bar and drew two pints of Harp. He put them on the bar, picked up the tab, rang it up and put it back in front of the drinkers. Then he moved back to Jesse.

"How come you're asking?" he said.

"Just making conversation," Jesse said.

Doc squinted at Jesse and shrugged. "Yeah, you're a big conversation maker," he said.

"I try," Jesse said.

He got up from the bar and went to a pay phone and called the station.

"Anthony? Jesse. You know those Hopkins kids, torched the house on Geary Street? Well, I want a cruiser to park outside their house for a half hour every shift, starting tonight. No, don't say anything, don't do anything. Just park outside the house a half hour every shift. That's right. I want to make them nervous."

chapter 8

At 2:15 in the afternoon, Macklin was sipping a Kettle One martini with a twist, at a sports bar on Huntington Avenue. He was wearing baggy olive linen slacks with three reverse pleats, a loose-fitting black silk tee shirt, and alligator loafers with no socks. In his wallet he had ten one hundred-dollar bills from Faye's savings account. In his pants pocket, he had a hundred and a twenty left from the liquor store.

There were four people besides Macklin in the room: a man and woman at a table eating buffalo wings, and a white-haired man down the bar, watching the soccer game that was on every big screen television in the room. The bartender was slicing lemons.

"Quiet afternoon," Macklin said.

"Usually is," the bartender said, "this time on a weekday." He was a middle-sized young guy with a thick moustache.

"Soccer don't help," Macklin said.

"Some people like it," the bartender said. "Can't get into it myself."

"Whaddya like?" Macklin said.

"Football," the bartender said.

"Now you're talking," Macklin said. "You bet?"

"Sure," the bartender said. "Last year I was up about a bill and a half."

He finished slicing the lemons and put them in a jar and put the jar in the refrigerator under the counter. Then he came down the bar and nodded at Macklin's glass.

"Buy you one?" he said.

"Be a fool not to say yes," Macklin answered.

The bartender scooped some ice into a shaker. Without measuring, he poured in vodka and a splash of vermouth.

"You must know the game," Macklin said. "Come out ahead."

The bartender rattled the martini around in the shaker and then poured it through the strainer into a chilled glass.

"I played some in high school," he said. "And I pay attention."

He ran a twist of lemon around the rim of the glass and then dropped it into the martini.

"Makes the game more interesting," Macklin said, "you got something on it."

"You got that right."

Macklin sipped his second martini. "Nice job," he said to the bartender.

The bartender grinned and went down the bar to the white-haired man. Macklin took the hundred from his pocket and put it on the bar. The bartender poured a double shot of Jack Daniels over some ice and put it on a paper napkin in front of the man. Then he strolled back up the bar to Macklin. He gave no indication that he saw the hundred.

"I'm from out of town," Macklin said. "And I'm bored. You know where I could find a card game?"

"Where you from?"

"Dannemora, New York," Macklin said.

"And you want to play poker?"

"Yeah. Good game. Some money changing hands, you know?"

"Sure," the bartender said. "Lemme make a call."

The bartender went down the bar and punched out a number on the phone. He talked for a moment and then hung up and walked back down to Macklin.

"You know the Lincolnshire Hotel?"

Macklin shook his head.

"You can walk there. You call Tommy King from the lobby. Tell him Lennie Seltzer sent you. They'll tell you the room number and up you go."

"You Lennie?"

"No, Lennie's the guy I called."

"Excellent," Macklin said. "How do I get there?"

He finished his second martini while the bartender gave him directions. Then he got up, left the hundred on the bar and headed for the door.

"Wish me luck," he said.

The bartender gave him a thumbs-up, and Macklin went out onto Huntington Avenue and walked to the Copley Place Garage where he had parked his car. He took the thousand dollars from his wallet and crumpled the bills and put them in his right-hand pants pocket. Inside the car, he unlocked the glove compartment and took out his 9-mm pistol. He undid his pants. Instead of shorts, he was wearing an oversized jock with a cup. He shoved the pistol down inside the cup. He took a roll of adhesive tape from the glove compartment, tore off some, and taped the handle of the gun against his belly, well below the navel. Then he got out and tucked in his shirt and buttoned his pants. He locked the car and cut through Copley Place on his way to the hotel. He paused outside a leather goods store and looked at himself reflected in the dark glass of the display window. The gun didn't show, just as it hadn't shown when he rehearsed this morning.

It was a perfect summer day in Boston as Macklin strolled through the Back Bay. He didn't need the directions. He knew where the Lincolnshire was. Inside the ornate lobby, he called Tommy King on an ivory house phone.

"Name's Hoyle," Macklin said. "Lennie Seltzer sent me."

"Room four-eighteen."

"I'll be up," Macklin said.

The elevator smelled of lilacs. The corridor was done in dark red carpet and ivory woodwork. The numbers on the doors were done in gold. At room 418 Macklin stopped. The emergency exit was two doors beyond— out the door and turn left. He rang the little illuminated bell beside the door. When the door opened, he stepped into a small foyer. Room 418 was in fact a two-bedroom suite.

In the foyer with him was a big man with thick hands.

"Mr. Hoyle?"

"That's me," Macklin said.

"Sorry, sir, but I'll have to pat you down. Just routine."

A short plump man in a white silk shirt was standing behind the big man. He had thin black hair plastered against his balding skull.

"Sergeant Voss is an off-duty police officer," the plump man said. "Just to make sure everything's on the up and up."

"Excellent," Macklin said. "Makes me feel safe."

He spread his arms and stood straight while Sergeant Voss ran his hands under each arm, down each side, around Macklin's belt line, and down each leg. Sergeant Voss was assiduous, as Macklin knew he would be, in avoiding Macklin's crotch. When he was through, Sergeant Voss stepped back and nodded at the plump man.

"I'm Tommy King," the plump man said. "Come on in."

The game was in the living room. Five men at a round table, with a sixth chair waiting for Macklin at the sixth spot. A blond woman with prominent breasts and a short black dress was overseeing the buffet and bar that was set up at the far end of the living room.

"Drink?" King said.

"I'll just take a beer," Macklin said. "Maybe a shrimp cocktail."

"Fine. Tiffany will get it for you. "

Macklin sat down. He took the thousand out of his pants pocket and put it on the table beside him without making much attempt to smooth them out.

"The gentleman with the five-o'clock shadow is Tony, my dealer."

Macklin nodded at him.

"The rest will introduce themselves," King said.

"Bill," the first player said, and they went around the table.

"Chuck."

"Mel."

"John."

"Sully."

Macklin smiled and nodded. Tiffany brought him beer and shrimp cocktail and managed to rub one of her breasts against him as she did so.

"Five-card draw," Tony said. "Jacks or better. Hundred-dollar minimum."

Macklin nodded and put his hundred in the pot. Tony began to deal. He was thin with dense black hair that waved straight back. The cards seemed to move about in his thin hands as if they were alive. Macklin got a pair of threes. Chuck opened. Macklin drew three cards. It didn't improve his threes. He dropped out. Chuck won with three queens. Tiffany made sure everyone had what they needed in food and drink. And she made sure that she rubbed her chest against all the players but Tony. Tony neither ate nor drank. Sergeant Voss leaned on the wall in the foyer. Occasionally Tommy King sat in for Tony. Macklin was a competent card player, but it didn't interest him. Gambling was for losers. There were better ways to get money. And there were better ways to lose it . . . like women. Macklin played hard enough to make it seem he was trying and kept close track of the amount of money that was moving across the table.

After an hour and a half, Macklin was down $200.

"Excuse me a minute," he said. "Damn beer, you don't drink it, you just rent it."

He stood and walked through a bedroom into the bath and closed the door and locked it. Then he unbuttoned his pants, pulled the tape off the gun butt and took the pistol out of his protector. He put the pistol down on the top of the toilet tank and took the occasion to urinate. Make it authentic. Then he zipped up. Washed his hands, dried them on a towel, picked up the pistol, cocked it, and went back through the bedroom. He took a pillow off the bed and shook the pillowcase loose. Carrying it in his left hand, with the 9-mm in his right, he went into the poker room. The first thing he did as he stepped through the bed-room door was to shoot Sergeant Voss in the middle of the chest. Voss grunted and fell on his left side and twitched a couple of times and was still. It took the starch out of everyone else in the room. Macklin waved the gun gently toward the poker players. Tiffany began to cry softly. Macklin ignored her.

"Any one of you can be next," Macklin said. "Unless I get all the money."

Nobody spoke.

"Everybody clasp their hands behind their head."

They did as they were told.

"No problem," Tommy King said. "You'll get your money."

"This is true," Macklin said. "Now, one by one, starting with you, Tommy, get up, empty your pockets into the pil-lowcase. And then lie facedown on the floor," he gestured with the gun barrel, "right there."

They did as they were told. After all the men had done as they were told, Macklin picked up the money on the table and handed it to Tiffany.

"Hold that," he said.

Then he surveyed the room.

"In a minute I'm going to search you, one at a time. If I find you held out on me, I'm going to shoot you in the back of the head."

He paused a moment.

"Anybody got anything to declare?"

Nobody moved. Macklin grinned. "Okay, I believe you. Come on, Tiffany."

He took hold of her wrist and led her past the dead man in the foyer and out the front door. Turn left. Two doors down. Into the emergency stairwell. Tiffany was still crying. He let go of her.

"I left you behind, they'd have taken the money away from you," he said. "Now you're on your own."

And he left her clutching the table stakes and sniveling, and he ran down the four flights. At the bottom he took the gun off cock, dropped it in the pillowcase, and went out the emergency door onto the street.

chapter 9

"So now you're a weather weenie," Jesse said.

He sat at the counter in Jenn's kitchen in a newly remodeled third-floor condominium on Beacon Street. Jenn had shown him around. From her bedroom window, you could see the Charles River. He had felt uneasy in her bedroom, but he was more comfortable now, sipping a scotch and soda, while Jenn transferred supper from the take-out boxes to the plates.

"Only the guys have to be weenies," Jenn said. "The weather girls have to look," she stuck out her chest and wiggled her hips, "goooood."

Jesse smiled.

"What about 'having a film career'?"

Jenn shook her head. "Have to ball too many toads," she said.

"Like Elliot?" Jesse said.

"Yeah, and the worst part is after you ball them, they're still toads."

She had bought chicken salad at the take-out, and cold

sesame noodles, and a loaf of sourdough bread. She went to the refrigerator and took out a bottle of Chardonnay and handed it to Jesse.

"Opener's right there beside the wine bucket," she said.

Jesse finished his scotch, opened the wine, and poured two glasses. He handed one to Jenn as she came around the counter to sit beside him. She touched his glass with hers.

"I don't know what to drink to," Jesse said.

"We could drink to each other."

"Okay," Jesse said. They drank.

"So," Jesse said. "Here we are."

"Yes."

"But I don't quite know where here is."

"Other than three thousand miles from Los Angeles?" She served a spoonful of chicken salad onto his plate.

"It's got grapes in it," Jesse said.

"That makes it chicken salad Veronique."

Jenn served him some sesame noodles and took some for herself. She liked to eat, and she was careful about what she ate. But she put together some very odd combinations, Jesse thought. Sesame noodles and chicken salad? Veronique? She was sitting beside him eating neatly. She seemed calm. He could smell her perfume, and he could brush her arm if he leaned slightly left. He remembered exactly what she looked like with her clothes off. He felt as if he might come apart and scatter on her kitchen floor. He sipped some Chardonnay. He didn't like wine that much. He particularly didn't like Chardonnay. But he knew she always had ordered it when they were married, and this had been the most expensive bottle of Chardonnay in the Cove Liquor Store, which was the nearest liquor store to the police station.

"You doing good with your drinking, Jesse?"

"I'm all right, Jenn. I slip occasionally, but never in public."

"Drinking alone?"

"Yep. But not often."

"I worry about you drinking alone."

"Hell, I've always liked drinking alone, Jenn. I hate being drunk where people can see me."

"I know. You're a very inward person."

Jenn was eating her noodles with chopsticks. He admired how clever she was with the chopsticks. He always used a fork. She ate some noodles, put down the chopsticks, drank some wine.

"Well," she said. "The question is where are we."

Jesse nodded. He wasn't hungry. He drank some wine.

"I've had quite a lot of therapy since we broke up," she said.

"We didn't break up," Jesse said. "You left me for Elliot the producer."

Jenn nodded carefully.

"I've had quite a bit of therapy since I took up with Elliot Krueger and you divorced me," she said.

"I'm sorry," Jesse said. "I guess I'm quibbling over language."

"You're mad," Jenn said. "And why wouldn't you be?"

"You did what you had to do."

"I guess so," Jenn said. "But all the therapy I've had hasn't solved my problem."

"Which is?"

"I want to be with you and I don't."

"And what's the shrink say about that?"

"She says I'm ambivalent."

"For this she gets a hundred dollars an hour?"

"Two hundred. And she's worth it. She helped me see that I really feel both ways at the same time, that it's really quite human to feel conflicting things."

"So what do you do about it?"

"I don't know yet. But I know I want to stay near you. You were too far away before."

"And what do we do with your ambivalence? You fuck me on Mondays and Wednesdays, and Elliot Tuesdays and Thursdays?"

"It's not about fucking, Jesse."

"The hell it isn't."

"Well. It's not only about fucking."

Jesse took in some air. He finished his wine. Better not have any more.

"Okay," he said, "it's not only about fucking. It's about you don't want me and you don't want to lose me. What the Christ am I supposed to do with that?"

"Talk."

"That's what I'm doing."

"No," Jenn said. "Mostly you're yelling."

Jesse got off the stool and walked into Jenn's frilly living room and looked down at Beacon Street.

"Goddamn, this is hard," he said.

She stood in the doorway behind him. "It's awful, isn't it?" she said.

"Yes."

"Dr. St. Claire says the bond between us is quite impressive."

Jesse nodded, staring down at the cars outbound toward Kenmore Square.

"I think we need to try," Jenn said.

"Try what?" Jesse said.

"Jesse," Jenn said. "We're divorced. We're single. We can act like any other single people. We could date."

"Date who?"

"Anybody we wanted," Jenn said. "Including each other. Like we'd just met."

"And?" Jesse said.

"And see what happens."

"Sex?" Jesse said.

Jenn shrugged. "Let's see what happens."

"Not tonight," Jesse said.

"No," Jenn said.

Jesse turned from the window and looked at Jenn and smiled.

"You are a piece of work, Jenn," he said.

"You want to give it a try?"

"Sure," Jesse said.

"Want to take me to dinner next Wednesday night?"

"Yes."

They stood on opposite sides of the living room for a

time and looked silently at each other. Then Jenn walked across and put her arms around Jesse and rested her head against his chest.

With her voice somewhat muffled, she said, "A day at a time, huh?"

"Sure," Jesse said.

chapter 10

"And you just walked out and shot the cop without a word," Faye said.

They were sitting in the Mercedes parked on Indian Hill, looking at Stiles Island where it jutted into the harbor.

"He was the dangerous one. Knock him over and they take you seriously."

"So you did it for effect."

"I wanted to neutralize him. And I wanted to get their attention."

"Weren't you afraid someone would hear the shot?" Faye said.

"Hotel rooms have pretty good sound insulation," Macklin said. "And most people don't know what a gun shot sounds like anyway. They're afraid to call up and make an asshole of themselves, you know?"

"Why didn't they call down to the desk the minute you left the room?"

"And say what—we were having an illegal poker game up here, guarded by a corrupt Boston cop? As soon as I left the room, they were busy getting the hell out of there and covering their tracks."

"So they won't even report it."

"Nope. Why I like to knock them over."

"Paper says that a policeman was found shot to death in a room," Faye said.

"And the room was occupied by someone named Thomas King, who turns out to be a phony."

"It didn't say in the paper."

"It will," Macklin said. "The real Thomas King will be a guy from Des Moines, who's never been to Boston, and somebody lifted his credit card number and used it to make phony plastic."

"You take some awful chances, Jimmy."

"Not really," Macklin said.

"What if the cop had found your gun?"

"Guy's patting you down he stays away from your crotch."

"But suppose he had found it?"

"So he takes it," Macklin said. "And they either boot me out or let me play. If they boot me out, I take my thousand and leave. If they let me play, I donate my thousand and leave."

"But shooting the cop?"

"Part of doing business," Macklin said. "Either it bothers you or it doesn't. If it bothers you, find another line of work."

"It doesn't bother you."

"No."

"What if you'd missed?"

Macklin grinned at her.

"I don't miss."

They were quiet. Below them, a sloop, heeling sharply in the offshore wind, was moving out of the harbor under sail. They were too far to make out the people onboard.

"So how much did you get?" Faye said.

"Fifteen thousand and change," Macklin said. "Should keep us afloat until we clean out Stiles Island."

"You really think we can?"

"It's perfect," Macklin said. "The isolation. The money. The police."

"Small-town cops?"

"You bet," Macklin said. "Biggest robbery they've ever had is probably some kid copping two Snickers bars from a Ma and Pa."

"I think something happened here last year, while you were in jail."

"Probably caught a Peeping Tom," Macklin said.

"No—I don't remember. It was on the news one night."

"Whatever," Macklin said and grinned at her again. "They haven't seen anything like me before."

Faye smiled back at him. "Not many people have," she said.

chapter 11

Suitcase Simpson and Anthony DeAngelo brought the Hopkins boys and Snapper Jencks in to see Jesse at 9:15 in the morning. None of them seemed scared. They all seemed to enjoy the celebrity of being arrested.

"Nobody was home but the kids," DeAngelo said. "Either house. I left a note."

"My father's going to be down here with a lawyer soon as he finds out," Earl said.

Jesse nodded. Simpson closed the door and leaned against it.

"I don't think you're supposed to arrest a kid without his parents' permission anyway," Robbie said. "You better call my mother at work."

Jesse leaned back in his chair and looked at them with the dead-eyed cop look he'd polished to a gleaming edge in South Central L.A. He let his eyes move slowly from one to the other, letting his gaze rest heavily on each of them. Jencks was the hard case. He met Jesse's look. The other two didn't. Jesse looked at Earl.

"You want a lawyer?" Jesse said.

"I don't know no lawyer," Earl said.

"Want me to get you one?"

"I don't want your lawyer," Earl said. "You better wait until my old man gets here."

"How old are you?" Jesse said.

"Fifteen."

Jesse looked at Robbie.

"You?" he said.

"Fourteen."

"You?" he said to Jencks.

"Old enough," Jencks said.

Jesse nodded. Jencks looked older than the other two. He was short, but he already had the shadow of a beard, and he had muscle definition. Didn't have to be older. Might merely have grown up quicker.

"Here's how it's going to go," Jesse said.

"You better let me call my mother or father," Earl said.

Jesse gestured at the phone. Earl stared at it and didn't call. Jesse hadn't thought he would. They weren't scared enough yet, and they didn't want their parents to know they were in trouble. Yet.

"Shut up," Jesse said. "We're going to ask you to wait in separate cells while we question you one at a time until one of you tells us that the three of you set the fire on Geary Street. Then we will throw the book at the ones who held out on us and go easy on the one who cooperated."

"Think you're bad," Earl said, "picking on three kids?"

"This the toughest we got?" Jesse said to Simpson.

"Three of the toughest kids in Paradise," Simpson said.

"How you think they'll do at Lancaster?" Jesse said.

Simpson and DeAngelo both laughed.

"They were in with the girls," he said, "they'd be the three sissies."

Jesse nodded.

"You think you're tough because kids in the schoolyard are scared of you, and you dare do things like torch somebody's house. Small town tough guys." He snorted. "But when we send you up, you'll be in with people who routinely carry razor blades in their hat bands, who would cut you right across the eyeballs for a pack of cigarettes, or for the hell of it. They will have you snowflakes for a snack."

Earl said, "I want . . ."

And Jesse cut him off. "I don't care what you want," Jesse said. "Get them out of here, Suit." Simpson and DeAngelo left with the three kids. In ten minutes Simpson came back.

"The Hopkins kids are scared already," he said. "I could see it when we put them in their cells. Jencks is the tough one."

"Yeah," Jesse said. "I know. "

"We don't have too long, Jesse," Simpson said. "One of the parents will come home from work or get a call from a neighbor, or whatever, and they'll be up here with a lawyer."

"We'll make do," Jesse said. "You got them isolated?"

"Yeah."

"Leave the cell doors unlocked?"

"Yeah."

"They know that?"

"No."

Jesse smiled.

"Jencks in the farthest cell?"

"Yeah."

"Okay," Jesse said, "bring him in here. Make sure they both see him on the way by."

When Jencks was in Jesse's office, Jesse nodded Simpson from the room and pointed at the empty chair in front of his desk. Jencks sat.

He met Jesse's look.

"You're not scared?" Jesse said.

Jencks shook his head.

"I'm a juvenile," Jencks said. "You can't do shit with me."

"You know one of the Hopkins boys will rat you out," Jesse said.

"Nobody's gonna rat nobody," Jencks said.

Jesse smiled and shook his head.

"You gonna be a bad guy, Snapper, you better learn the business. Everybody rats everybody. It's only a matter of time and pressure."

Jencks leaned back in his chair and clasped his hands behind his head and stared at Jesse without speaking. He had on baggy jeans and big sneakers. He wore a Foo Fighters sweatshirt. Jesse assumed that Foo Fighters was a rock group.

"You're a tough kid," Jesse said. "I like that. Why I gave you the first shot. You tell me about the fire and you walk."

"Even if I did it too?"

"Two out of three ain't bad," Jesse said.

"Some great legal system," Jencks said.

"Here's how I think it went," Jesse said. "The three of you started out just busting in there because the place was empty. And you didn't have anything else going. Then you got in there and decided it would be fun to write 'fag' on the walls, and then one of the Hopkins boys, Earl, I bet, said, 'Let's torch the fucker.' I figure you didn't much want to because you thought it was stupid, but you went along because they were going to do it anyway. You may have even tried to stop them but couldn't."

"I wanted to stop them, they'd stop," Jencks said.

Jesse nodded. "Yeah, I can see that," Jesse said. "I'm surprised you wanted to do it too. Go to jail for what? No money in it. Just a kid's asshole prank. I figured you for a little more serious tough guy than that."

"Showed them fairies something," Jencks said.

"What'd you show them, tough guy?"

"Showed 'em," Jencks said stubbornly.

Jesse laughed. His laugh was rich with contempt.

"Sure," Jesse said. "One time, and one time only, you want to tell me what happened and walk, or you want to go to jail?"

"I ain't going to jail."

"Yeah, you are," Jesse said. "And because you're so fucking stupid, you may be the only one." Jesse raised his voice. "Suit?"

Simpson opened the door.

"Take him out," Jesse said. "Turn him loose."

Jencks looked startled.

"Back way?" Simpson said.

"Yeah."

"Come on," Simpson said, and he led Jencks out of Jesse's office. In two minutes he was back.

"They see him go?" Jesse said.

"Yeah. I took him down past the cells," Simpson said, "with my arm around his shoulder. When I let him out the back door, I shook hands with him. They could see all that."

"Okay," Jesse said. "Go get the younger one."

"Robbie."

"Yeah. Arrest him. Read him his rights. Cuff him in front."

Seated in the chair, his cuffed hands resting in his lap, Robbie was very pale and swallowed often. Jesse ignored him while he read some documents on his desk. He initialed one and picked up another, read it initialed it and put it in his out basket.

"I don't like these handcuffs," Robbie said.

"I don't care," Jesse said without looking up. He studied the next document for a moment, shook his head, and put it in another pile.

"Couldn't you please take them off?"

Jesse read for another moment, then, still holding the document, he looked up at Robbie.

"You think I'm your camp counselor or something?" Jesse said. "We got you for a felony, kid. You're going to jail."

"I didn't do anything," Robbie said. His voice was clogged, and Jesse knew he'd cry in a little while. "I don't like these handcuffs."

"First thing to know," Jesse said, "now that you are officially a tough guy, is that from now on nobody will give one small shit about what you like and don't like. You're not home with your momma. You're in the machine now, boy. You want me to get you a lawyer?"

Jesse went back to his paper work. Robbie stared at him, and when he spoke again his voice was shaking and his eyes were wet.

"But I didn't do anything," he said.

"Not how I hear it," Jesse said absently, scanning a missing persons flyer. "Heard you did the spray painting. Heard you actually poured the gasoline and struck the match."

"No." Robbie's voice was shrill now.

"Snapper and Earl were only in the house in the first place because they were trying to get you out. They both tried to stop you, but they were too late."

Robbie was crying now. There was a tape recorder on Jesse's desk. Jesse punched the RECORD button.

"No," Robbie said, struggling to talk through the sobs. "No. I wasn't even in the house. I was outside watching chickie for the cops."

"Oh? So who set the fire?"

"I don't know. I wasn't even in there. Earl had the gas can."

"You're trying to tell me that he was in there with Snapper?"

"Snapper told us he found an open window at the fag house and he'd been in there and tagged the walls in the living room," Robbie said. He was talking as fast as he could, at the same time struggling not to wail. "Earl stole the gas from my dad, for the power mower, and him and Snapper told me to watch for the cops, and they went in the house."

"Through the window?"

"No, Snapper left the door unlocked."

"And you went in and torched the place," Jesse said gently.

"No," Robbie almost screamed. "No, I didn't. Snapper and Earl torched it."

Jesse punched the STOP button on his tape recorder. Then he got up and went around the desk and took the cuffs off Robbie's wrists. He shoved a box of tissues to the edge of the desk where Robbie could reach it and went back and sat down. He raised his voice.

"Suitcase?"

The door opened. And Simpson appeared.

"Time to talk with Earl," Jesse said.

chapter 12

Macklin was having lunch outside on the patio at Janos restaurant in Tucson with an Indian named Crow. The Indian's real name was Wilson Cromartie, but he liked to be called Crow. He was wearing a short-sleeved white shirt, pressed blue jeans, polished boots, and a silver concho belt. Everything about Crow was angles and planes, as if he had been packed very tightly into himself. The muscles bulged against his taut skin like sharp corners. The veins were prominent. He wasn't much bigger than Macklin, but everything about him spoke of force tightly compressed. They were drinking margaritas.

"And you want me to be the shooter?" Crow said.

"Not just a shooter," Macklin said. "I need a force guy, somebody can do the job on the operation and keep discipline in the crew."

"You can't do that?"

"I can do that, but I gotta run the whole dance, you know? Besides I don't scare people like you do."

"That's 'cause you look like some guy graduated Cornell," Crow said.

His voice had traces of that indefinable Indian overtone, even though Macklin knew that Crow hadn't seen a rain dance in his entire life.

"And I sound like it, and that works pretty good for me. But I still need a force guy."

"And you come all the way to Tucson to hire me?" Crow said.

"To cut you in," Macklin said. "I'm trying to cut you in on the score of a fucking lifetime and you're asking questions like I was trying to steal your land."

"White eyes speak with forked tongue," Crow said.

"Don't give me that Geronimo crap," Macklin said. "It's me, Jimmy Macklin. You wouldn't know a tepee from a pee pee, for crissake."

Crow's expression didn't change.

"Tepee bigger," he said.

A waitress came and took their lunch order. There were small birds in some dry desert shrubbery around the patio. They made a lot of noise.

When the waitress left, Crow said, "Twenty percent."

"I got too many expenses, Crow. I gotta get an electronics guy, explosives guy, guy with a boat. I can't afford to give you twenty."

"How much you taking?"

"Half," Macklin said. "My show."

"And I'm the number-two man?"

"Absolutely."

"Twenty," Crow said.

"That only leaves thirty percent for everybody else," Macklin said. "I can't get quality guys divvying thirty."

"Lie to them," Crow said.

Macklin grinned.

"How you know I promise you twenty, I'm not lying to you?"

"You know better," Crow said.

Macklin cocked a forefinger at Crow and brought the thumb down.

"Twenty it is," Macklin said.

chapter 13

Abby Taylor was in Jesse's office with another lawyer.

"I've been retained to represent Carleton Jencks," Abby said. "This is Brendan Fogarty, who represents the Hopkins boys."

Abby had on a maroon suit with a short skirt and a short jacket with no lapels.

"You a criminal lawyer, Mr. Fogarty?" Jesse said.

"I'm Charles Hopkins' personal attorney," Fogarty said.

"This is a criminal case," Jesse said.

"Well," Abby said, "that's what we wanted to talk about."

Abby would be wearing maroon lingerie. When he had been in a position to know such things, her undergarments had always been coordinated.

"Go ahead," Jesse said.

"These are kids," Abby said. "They made a mistake, but they have a life ahead of them. To press charges will just make matters worse."

"You talk to Canton and Brown?" Jesse said.

"Yes. They came to me to ask if I could represent them in a civil suit, but I had already been retained by the Jencks family."

"They don't want to press charges?"

"The Jencks family and, as I believe Mr. Fogarty will confirm, the Hopkins family are prepared to make financial restitution."

"If charges are dropped?"

"That would be the idea," Fogarty said.

"And what about the kids?" Jesse said.

"They get a second chance."

"To burn somebody else's house down?"

"They're kids, Jesse."

"And they burned down a house because they don't like the sex lives of the people who live there. What if they don't like your sex life?"

Jesse thought that Abby blushed faintly, but maybe he was wrong.

"Wait a minute, Jesse," Fogarty said.

"You don't know me," Jesse said. "Call me Chief Stone."

"Don't get hard-assed with me, chief," Fogarty said. "You don't have a case will stand up in court. You didn't read them their Miranda rights."

"They were read their rights when they were arrested," Jesse said. "They confessed."

"Under coercion. Questioned without an attorney. Thrown in a cell."

Peripherally, Jesse saw Abby shake her head at Fogarty. "This is not a big building, Mr. Fogarty. I needed to talk to each of them alone. There was nowhere else to put them. Cell door wasn't even locked. I offered them an attorney at every juncture."

"Handcuffed?"

"Once charged," Jesse said.

"You led them to believe that Jencks had implicated them," Fogarty said.

"That I did," Jesse said.

"You pretended to let him go, in order to reinforce that belief."

"Yes, I did," Jesse said. "He walked out the back door and sat in the patrol car for an hour with Anthony DeAngelo."

"There is a conscious pattern of deception and coercion of three minors," Fogarty said. "You better deal."

Abby shook her head again more vigorously. She knew that Fogarty's tactics wouldn't work with Jesse.

"I think your case may be shaky, Jesse," Abby said. "But that's not really the point. The point is do you want to put these kids and their families through this? The parents make restitution. The two gay gentlemen rebuild the house. Life goes on."

"And the 'two gay gentlemen'? How do they feel?"

"They got their house rebuilt," Fogarty said.

"People ought to be able to fuck who they want to," Jesse said. "Without getting their house burned down."

Abby knew Jesse was stubborn. But she had rarely seen him mad too.

"And you're going to fix that by running three kids and their families through the criminal courts?"

"I'm going to run them through the courts," Jesse said.

"To prove?" Abby said.

"That the kids can't mistreat whoever they want and have their parents buy them out of it."

The two lawyers were quiet. Abby knew it was a lost cause. Fogarty tried again.

"You won't get the DA into court with this," Fogarty said.

Jesse didn't reply.

"You'll look like a fool," Fogarty said. "You don't have a case."

"No disrespect, counselor," Jesse said. "But I guess I'm not willing to take your word on that."

chapter 14

There was a large photograph of Ozzie Smith on the wall in Jesse's living room where you could see it while sitting at the kitchen counter. Jesse looked at the photo as he poured soda over the ice in a tall glass of scotch. He took a drink. If you didn't drink, Jesse thought, you'd never get it. You'd never know the way it felt. Casual drinkers, people who drank to be sociable, who would just as soon have a 7UP if it weren't so unsophisticated, they couldn't understand the fuss about the first drink. Jesse had always thought that the first couple of drinks were like life itself. Pleasing, smooth, bubbly, and harsh. For people who didn't like the taste, Jesse had unaffected scorn. The greatest pleasure came long before you got drunk. After the first one, with the certainty of more, there was gratitude for the life you led. After a couple of drinks, the magic went away, and pretty soon it was just addiction.

"Got to work on that addiction," Jesse said to Ozzie Smith.

Ozzie was in midair, parallel to the ground, his glove

outstretched. As far as Jesse knew, Ozzie Smith had no addictions. Best shortstop that ever lived, Jesse said to himself. He knew it was too large a claim. He knew that Ozzie Smith was only the best shortstop he'd ever seen. He couldn't speak of Marty Marion or Pee Wee Reese, or for that matter, Honus Wagner. He drank some more scotch. They better than Ozzie, they were very god-damned good. He was pretty certain that none of the others did a back flip.

"Wizard of Oz," Jesse said out loud.

If he hadn't gotten hurt, he'd have made the show. He knew that somatically. He had always known he was a big-league shortstop. If he hadn't gotten hurt, he'd be just finishing up a career. Maybe moved to third in the last couple of years. Hit .275–.280 lifetime. Ten, twelve home runs. Less average maybe than Ozzie Smith, but a little more power. Good numbers for a guy with his glove. Guy who could throw a seed from the hole. His glass was empty. He went to the refrigerator, got more ice, and mixed himself another. He drank. Yes. Still there.

He'd made the show, he wouldn't be bullying teenagers for a living. "A conscious pattern of deception and coercion." Fogarty had that right. May not stand up in court. Depends on which judge they drew. Might not get to court. Depended on which prosecutor they drew. He wondered who Jenn might be sleeping with. Experience would suggest the station manager. On the other hand, she said she'd changed. She said Dr. St. Claire had helped her be different than she was. Hard to love somebody sleeping with somebody else. Could be done though. He could do it. Hell, he was good at it.

"Nice to be good at something, Oz."

Hadn't worked with Abby either. She wasn't tough enough, but at least she'd been faithful. Jenn was tough enough. One out of two ain't bad. When he was nineteen, playing in Colorado, he'd been able to do a back flip, like Ozzie Smith, when he ran out to short at the start of a game. He made himself another drink and took a pull. It wasn't there any more, but he took it back to the counter with him anyway. The truth of it was of course that he hadn't loved Abby. He'd liked her, and he'd tried to love her because he wanted to move on from Jenn. But he couldn't. That was a grim thought, wasn't it? That he couldn't move on from Jenn? Jesus Christ! He'd better be able to. Or, maybe he wouldn't have to. Or, maybe he was drunk.

He looked up at the picture of Ozzie Smith, frozen in midair.

"It's a long season, Oz," Jesse said out loud.

He drank most of the rest of his glass.

"And it's not like football," he said.

He emptied his glass and stood and made a fresh drink and brought it to the counter. He drank some and made a gesture with his glass toward the picture.

"We play this game every day," he said and heard himself slush the S in "this."

chapter 15

Macklin was eating fried chicken and mashed potatoes with a cracker named JD Harter at the Horse Radish Grill on Powers Ferry Road in the Buckhead section of Atlanta.

"How big is big money?" JD said.

He was small and slim with thick black hair worn long enough to cover his ears and slicked straight back. He had a pointed nose and wore rose-tinted black-rimmed glasses. He was dressed in a powder blue jogging suit with dark maroon trim and a satin finish. On his feet were woven leather loafers and no socks.

"Everybody gets at least a million," Macklin said.

JD raised his eyebrows.

"Large," he said. "How much you get?"

"More than anybody else," Macklin said.

"Figures," JD said. "How much more?"

"Long as you get yours, what do you care?" Macklin said.

JD shrugged. "I expect to get fucked," he said. "Just like to know how bad."

Macklin grinned.

"Chicken's great, isn't it?" JD said. He was drinking Coca-Cola with his bourbon.

"It is," Macklin said.

"What happens if I sign up, and after it's over I don't get no million?" JD said. "What kinda recourse I got?"

"You can try to kill me," Macklin said.

JD was silent for a moment. During the silence he drank more bourbon and chased it with more Coke. Then he said, "That'd be recourse, all right."

"You in?" Macklin said.

"Exactly what kinda electrical work you need done?" JD said.

"Alarms, phones, time locks, power lines, can't say for sure yet, partly because I need you to tell me."

JD nodded. "Who else you got?"

"Faye's with me."

"I'll be damned," JD said.

"And Crow," Macklin said.

"The Indian?"

"Yes."

"Well, by God, you are serious, ain't you."

"Nothing but the best," Macklin said. "Why I'm down here talking to you."

"Shi-it," JD said. "You going to toss anything but the bank?"

"Toss everything out there," Macklin said. "Bank, yacht club, health club, restaurant, real estate office, every house."

"For crissake, we going to move out there for the winter?"

"We'll make ourselves some time," Macklin said.

"I guess," JD said.

"So, you in?"

"I got any time to think about it?"

"No."

"I get to know where this island is?"

"Not until you need to."

"I need to now," JD said.

Macklin grinned at him again.

"I said it wrong, I meant not until *I* think you need to."

"You never going to get in trouble by blabbing, are you?" JD said.

"Probably not," Macklin said.

"Got to decide tonight, don't I?" JD said.

"You're not in by the time I leave the restaurant," Macklin said, "I cross you off and go see the next guy."

"I the first wire guy you asked?"

"Yes."

"Who's next?"

Macklin shook his head. JD took a drink of Wild Turkey and held it in his mouth for a time before he swallowed. He chased it with Coca-Cola.

"What's your problem, JD?" Macklin said. "I'm giving you a shot at easy street the rest of your life. What's holding you up?"

The waitress came and cleared the table and gave them dessert menus. JD scanned his.

"Peach pie," he said. "That's for me."

Macklin glanced at his menu and put it down and, with his elbows on the table, rested his chin on his folded hands. He let his gaze rest on JD. And he waited.

"You want the peach pie?" JD said. "It's great here."

"Sure," Macklin said.

The waitress took their dessert order and went away.

"We're leveling with each other here. Right, Jimmy?" Macklin said, "Sure."

"I mean no disrespect here, but you've always cut things very sharp, you know?"

"Sharp?" Macklin said.

"I mean nobody ever quite knows what you're thinking, and you never quite say, and nothing's ever quite the way it looks like it is when you start."

"Faye knows what I'm thinking," Macklin said.

"Well that's nice, Jimmy. I'm glad she does. I really am. But nobody else does."

"You don't trust me," Macklin said.

"Well, not to put too fine a point on it, Jimmy, but, no. I don't."

"Well, JD," Macklin said, his chin still resting on his folded hands, "that's your problem."

"I know. I know you don't care. Man, it's part of what worries me. You don't care about nothing."

JD paused thinking about what he'd said.

"Except Faye," JD said.

Macklin waited. The waitress brought the dessert. When she left, JD stared at the pie for a moment and then sat back in his chair.

"Here's how it looks to me, Jimmy. I get into this with you, and I might get rich or I might get fucked. I don't get into this with you, I won't get rich, and, being as how I'm a crook, I may get fucked anyway."

Macklin waited. JD ate a forkful of pie.

"So I'm in," JD said.

"Good. How's the pie?"

"Excellent," JD said.

chapter 16

Jesse leaned on one elbow against the end of the bar at the yacht club and looked out over the water at the tip of Stiles Island. He had a scotch and soda in his hand. Around him the princes of Paradise danced with their princesses at the annual Race Regatta Cotillion to a band playing music from the Meyer Davis songbook. Jesse hated these events, and he hated them particularly when he had to go alone. It would go easier with a few drinks. But he couldn't let himself have a few drinks, and he hated fighting it off. But he was the chief of police, and he knew it would help him in his work to be part of the social fabric of the town. So he was there.

Morris Comden, the chairman of the board of selectmen, stopped at the bar to pick up a vodka and tonic and chat with Jesse.

"Always a nice party, isn't it, Jess?"

Comden was a short, square man with a strong chin and deep-set eyes. Jesse had never heard him say an intelligent word.

"Sure is, Morris."

Jesse hated being called Jess.

"Look at those ladies in their party dresses," Comden said. "I was a single man like yourself, Jess, I'd be sashaying a few of them around the floor, lemme tell ya."

"You and Mrs. Comden cut a pretty mean sashay," Jesse said.

Mrs. Comden was a thin-lipped woman, taller than her husband, who wore no makeup. There was always about her a look of perpetual outrage. The Comdens dancing was in fact, Jesse thought, a mean sight.

"What happened between you and that little lawyer lady?" Comden said. He sipped his vodka and tonic as he spoke.

"Abby? Wasn't in the cards, I guess," Jesse said.

Jesse turned his tall glass in his hands slowly. The longer he took between sips, the longer it would last. Comden had no such inhibition, and he gulped some more of his drink. If Morris was quick, Jesse thought, he could get it in and get another before he went back to his table. Jesse smiled to himself. *Takes one to know one.*

"Heard your ex-wife came east to be on the television," Comden said.

"She's doing weather," Jesse said, "on Channel Three."

"You ever see her?"

"Some."

They were quiet for a moment. Comden drank most of the rest of his drink in short quick swallows. Jesse knew that Comden wanted to ask if Jesse were sleeping with Jenn, but he couldn't think how to ask.

"Well," Comden said, "that must be odd, seeing her again after you been divorced and all, and you having another girlfriend. She been, ah, seeing anybody?"

"It's kind of odd," Jesse said.

Comden's eyes shifted, looking for the bartender. When he caught his eye he gestured for a refill.

"Yeah, I'll bet it's odd," Comden said.

The bartender set a fresh vodka and tonic up on the bar, and Comden grabbed it as if it were about to flop into the water.

"Odd," Jesse said.

"Damned odd."

Jesse nodded.

"Well, can't leave my bride alone too long," Comden said. "Good seeing you, Jess."

"Nice talking with you, Morry."

He knew Comden preferred to be called Morris. It was late summer, and the sun was still above the horizon. Its reflection made a long shimmer straight across the dark water of the harbor. In another half hour it would be gone, and the blue evening would begin to thicken. Jesse took a small sip of scotch. When he got home, if he felt like it, he could have a couple of real ones before he went to bed. A tall, good-looking woman with a nice tan came to the bar and ordered an Absolut martini up with extra olives. Jesse smiled at her. She looked maybe five years older than he was, with platinum blond hair and a lot of makeup very well applied. She wasn't wearing a wedding ring.

"Isn't this awful," the woman said.

"That martini will probably help," Jesse said.

"If I could have enough of them."

"And you can't?"

She smiled and shook her head.

"I'm here because it's sort of good for business to be seen here," she said. "Neither one of us can get drunk in public."

"You know my business?"

"Sure. You're the chief of police."

"And you?" Jesse said.

"I sell real estate on Stiles Island. I brought a couple of prospective clients, let them circulate, get a feel for their neighbors."

She was wearing a very simple black dress with thin straps, which seemed to whisper engagingly over her body when she moved. Jesse could tell she worked out.

"People from Stiles don't usually come to these things," Jesse said.

"I told them that, but they said they'd like to get a sense of the whole town."

"This may blow the sale," Jesse said.

"Well, they're circulating," the woman said. "We'll just play it as it lays."

She put out her hand.

"Marcy Campbell."

Jesse took her hand and shook it.

"Jesse Stone," he said.

She leaned her elbow next to him on the bar and looked at the dance floor. She was only a couple of inches shorter than he was. Her hair smelled the way he was sure violets would have smelled if he had ever actually smelled a violet, which he hadn't.

"You know what violets smell like?" he said.

"No. But I'd recognize champagne in a heartbeat," she said.

Jesse smiled. "I like your priorities," he said.

"Despite life's busy pace," she said, "it's always nice to stop and smell the booze."

Jesse smiled again and they were quiet watching the dancers moving about the floor. The band was playing "Tie a Yellow Ribbon 'Round the Old Oak Tree." Most of the men wore white dinner jackets. Most of the women were in floor-length gowns, some of which were in small floral patterns. Many with puffy shoulders and bows in unexpected places. It looked like an overaged frat party.

"My God, look at those dresses," Marcy said.

"Colorful."

"Look at this with the bow on her ass," Marcy said. "If you had an ass like that, would you call attention to it by putting a bow on it?"

"I'd rather not think about her ass," Jesse said.

Marcy laughed and took one of the olives from her martini and popped it in her mouth. Jesse took another controlled sip of his scotch.

"Wouldn't you think," Marcy said, "with all that money and all that time on their hands, nobody works, that these women could manage to look better than they do?"

"Well it's not like they all married Tom Selleck," Jesse said.

"I suppose," Marcy said. "But you know I sometimes

seriously think about it. I mean really look at these people. Dancing to dreadful music, wearing dreadful clothes, saying dreadful boring things. Can they possibly be having any fun?"

"Maybe they think it's fun," Jesse said.

"But . . ." Marcy shook her head. "Just imagine the impoverishment of their daily lives," she said. "If this is their recreation."

"Better than no recreation," Jesse said.

"But that's the sad part. They do this and think it's fun, and so they never have any actual fun. Can you imagine these people in bed?"

"Another thing I'd prefer not to think about," Jesse said.

"Most men, and women, lead lives of quiet desperation," Marcy said.

"That's a quote from someplace," Jesse said.

Marcy laughed.

"Henry David Thoreau," she said. "I modified it a little."

"How about yourself?"

"Me? My desperations are never quiet," Marcy said.

"What do you do for fun?"

"Eat," she said, "drink, work out, shop, travel, read, talk to interesting people, have sex."

"Bingo," Jesse said.

"We've found a common interest?" Marcy said.

"Anyone special?" Jesse said.

"That I have sex with?"

"Yes."

Marcy laughed. The laugh was genuine and quite big. He had already noticed that her face flushed slightly when she laughed.

"They're all special," she said.

"No husband?" Jesse said.

"Not anymore."

"Boyfriend?"

"Not currently. How about you?"

"I'm divorced," Jesse said.

"I knew that. Girlfriends?"

"Nope."

"Do you think we've stayed here long enough?" Marcy said.

"Yes."

"Then let's go somewhere and get a real drink."

"What about the clients?"

"They have their own car. I'll just say good-bye."

Jesse watched the way her hips moved under the smooth tight dress as she walked away from him across the dance floor carrying her martini. She spoke to a good-looking couple near the buffet table. They looked more Palm Beach than Stiles Island, Jesse thought. But maybe they were just summer people. The man kissed Marcy on the cheek, and she turned and came back across the dance floor. In a while, Jesse was pretty sure, he'd see that body without the intervening dress. The pressure of possibility, which had begun almost as soon as she had spoken to him, was now very strong. He didn't mind. He enjoyed the pressure. No hurry. He enjoyed looking forward to it. Marcy put her empty glass down on the bar.

"Shall we?" she said.

Jesse drained the rest of his drink and put his glass on the bar beside hers.

"You bet," Jesse said.

chapter 17

"See the guy over there talking to Marcy?" Macklin said.

"Cute," Faye said.

"What's so cute?" Macklin said.

"Well he's slim, but he looks strong. He's got a nice face. Good hair. Looks sort of, I don't know, graceful. He's cute."

"Whaddya think he does for a living?" Macklin said.

"He's some kind of professional athlete."

"He's the chief of police," Macklin said.

"He's young," she said. "How do you know he's the police chief?"

"I scoped out the police station, so's I can recognize the cops, and I see him come and go. Plain clothes, unmarked car, and he walks like, you know, 'This is mine.' So I go over the library and get a town report and look up the police department and there he is, Jesse Stone, chief of police."

"You don't miss much do you, Jimmy?" Faye's voice was admiring.

"No more than I have to."

He liked to think that of himself, Faye knew. He liked to think that he was prepared for everything. The truth was Faye knew that he simply enjoyed the foreplay. She had never said, *If you're so goddamned good why have you spent half your life in jail?* It would break his heart if he knew she thought less of him than he thought of himself. At least he was still alive. At least she still had him.

"How's he look to you aside from cute?" Macklin said.

"He looks like he might know what he's doing," Faye said.

"Why do you say that?"

"He looks different from all the other men here," Faye said. "And they clearly don't have any idea what they're doing."

Macklin laughed and put his arm around her shoulder. He turned her toward him, and they began to dance to "The Tennessee Waltz."

"Well, we're just going to fucking-A find that out, aren't we, my little chickadee?"

"Don't turn this into a game, Jimmy."

"A game?"

"Don't make this you against the cop to see who's better. Just steal the money and we'll go."

Macklin tightened his arms around her and held her against him. She rubbed her cheek gently against his.

"Not to worry," Macklin said. "We'll do the big knock-over and then we'll go someplace warm and sit beside each other and drink daiquiris in the sun."

"Yes," Faye said softly.

"You and me, babe," Macklin said.

"Yes."

"Always been you and me. Always will be."

Faye didn't say anything.

"Long time together, Faye," Macklin said.

"Just don't turn this into a game of chicken with the cop," Faye said.

"Don't worry," Macklin said. "I got this thing wired. We're going to do this right."

Faye didn't say anything else, as they moved across the dance floor. She kept her face pressed against his, and she closed her eyes.

chapter 18

They sat on the open deck of Marcy's small weathered shingle cottage on Strawberry Point in the east end of town, past the narrow harbor mouth, just above the buttress of rust-colored rocks against which the open Atlantic moved without respite. Jesse was drinking beer from the bottle. Marcy had a glass of white wine.

"I thought you drank scotch," Marcy said.

"I do, but beer's nice," Jesse said. "I thought you drank martinis."

"I do," Marcy said and smiled. "But wine is nice."

There were no lights on the deck, but there was a small moon and some starlight, and, as their eyes adjusted, they could see each other and the white spray of the breaking swells below them.

"You know why we were drinking differently at the yacht club?" Marcy said.

"Because we knew we couldn't drink many, so we were trying to get the most bang for the buck."

"I'll be damned," Marcy said. "You did know."

Jesse smiled. "I know a lot," he said.

"And so modest," Marcy said.

Jesse had his suit jacket off and it hung from the back of the chair to his left. Marcy could see the butt of his gun showing just in front of his right hip.

"You're carrying a gun," she said.

"I'm a cop."

"Do you always carry one?"

Jesse nodded.

"I'm always a cop," he said.

"What are you now?" she said.

Jesse drank from the bottle.

"Interested," he said.

They both laughed.

"First you," Marcy said. "Tell me about yourself."

"I was a cop in Los Angeles. I'm thirty-five and divorced."

"I'm older than you," Marcy said. "Always a cop?"

"No, I was a baseball player, before I got hurt."

"Did you play professionally?"

"Yes."

"Were you any good?"

"I was very good," Jesse said.

"How'd you get hurt?"

"On a double play at second, runner took me out, and I came down on my shoulder."

"What about the divorce?"

"I was married to a starlet," Jesse said. "She wanted to be a star, so she slept with producers."

"That start you drinking?"

"I used to tell myself it did," Jesse said. "But it didn't. I always liked to drink."

"But you have it under control now."

"Most of the time," Jesse said.

"You over the first wife?"

"No."

"You still love her?"

"Maybe."

"That must make it hard to commit to other women."

Jesse smiled. "Not for the short term."

Marcy smiled with him in the pale darkness.

"I've never met a man who couldn't commit for the short term," she said.

She sipped her wine. He drank some beer. Below them the ceaseless ocean moved hypnotically against the begrudging rocks.

"And I've met a lot," she said.

Jesse waited. It was her turn.

"You're honest," Marcy said. "Most men wouldn't have told me about the ex-wife and would have sworn they'd love me forever."

"So they could get you into bed," Jesse said.

"Yep."

"Doesn't mean I don't want that," Jesse said.

"No, I'm sure it doesn't," Marcy said. "But if I were husband hunting, and using my bed as bait, you'd have just blown the lay."

"Instead of vice versa," Jesse said.

Marcy laughed. And Jesse liked the way she laughed and joined in, and they both laughed as much for the pleasure of laughing together as for the bite of Jesse's wit.

"We'll see about vice versa," Marcy said.

"You looking for a husband?" Jesse said.

"No. I was married," she said. "At eighteen. I got two kids in college. Girl at Colby. Boy at Wesleyan."

"Lot of money," Jesse said.

"Their father can afford it."

"He supports them?"

"As always. I raised them. He paid for it. He's always been good that way."

"What way wasn't he good?"

"He was, is, a doctor. Very successful. A neurosurgeon. And he fucked every nurse that would hold still for twenty seconds."

"Like all the jokes," Jesse said.

"Like all the jokes," Marcy said. "He's not a bad man. He's generous, and he's a good father in his way. But where his penis leads, he follows."

"When'd you get divorced?"

"Ten years ago."

"You over it?"

"Yes."

"Want to get married again?"

"No."

Jesse finished the last of his beer and set it on the table beside him.

"Well," he said. "Hello."

"Hi."

They both laughed again. Marcy drank some wine.

"Here's the deal," she said. "I like men. I like wine. I like sex. Right now I'm having a nice time and I hope to have an even nicer one. I am not going to fall in love with you, and I don't think you'll fall in love with me. And, assuming you're interested, we can have some nice uncomplicated sex with nothing at stake. And we can be each other's friend."

Jesse leaned back in his chair and looked at her and said, "Works for me."

He kept looking at her in the semi-lucent darkness. She was quiet for a while as he did so, and then she said, "Assessing the goods?"

"No, well, maybe. I was just thinking how clear you are."

"I had a good shrink," Marcy said.

"The shrink had a good patient," Jesse said.

"Also true," Marcy said.

She stood and walked to the railing of her deck and placed her hips against it and sipped her drink.

"The trouble with being clear is that it makes the transitions a little awkward," she said. "I'm going to take a shower. Would you care to join me?"

"Sure," Jesse said.

chapter 19

"I need a boom guy," Macklin said.

He was leaning on a railing on the Baltimore waterfront looking across at the aquarium, talking to a tall, bony red-haired man named Fran.

"Uh-huh?" Fran said.

Fran wore small, round, gold-rimmed glasses. His wiry red hair was long and pulled back in a ponytail. He had on a short-sleeved green shirt and khaki pants and Hush Puppies. His bare arms were heavily freckled. He had a gold earring.

"You are the best around."

"True," Fran said. "What'd you have in mind?"

"I need a bridge blown."

"Legally?"

" 'Course not."

"What else?"

"Other things. I'll tell you when you need to know."

"Maybe I need to know to decide if I want the job."

"Job's worth more than a million."

"Total?"

"Each."

A water taxi pulled up to the dock below them and some tourists got out and headed up the stairs toward Harbor Place.

"Each is good," Fran said. "Who's in it?"

"So far, Crow, JD, Faye, and me," Macklin said.

"She waited for you."

"Yes."

Fran nodded.

"Where's this going to go down?" he said.

Macklin smiled and shook his head.

"Keep thinking about the million," Macklin said. "It's what you need to know."

"You wouldn't have Crow if you didn't think it would take some doing," Fran said.

"Better to have him and not need him," Macklin said, "than need him and not have him."

"Maybe," Fran said. "How many guys you need all together?"

"One more after you," Macklin said.

"I'm married now," Fran said.

"Congratulations."

"Four kids."

"How about that," Macklin said.

"I been legit since I got out. Working for the city, mostly slum clearance."

"Making the big buck?"

"Not this big," Fran said. "How long will it take?"

"You'll probably be gone a week, ten days."

"Ten days?"

"It's a big job. You'll need some time."

"Ten days," Fran said, "I could blow up Baltimore."

"You have to look at the site," Macklin said. "Decide what you need. Then you have to get it. And install it. It'll take some time. You can't get away ten days for a million bucks?"

"Old lady'll croak," Fran said. "I tell her I'm leaving her alone with four kids for ten days."

"You'll have to deal with your wife," Macklin said.

The two of them were silent then, their forearms resting on the railing, the littered sea water washing tamely against the pier. The harbor was busy with small boats and behind them Harbor Place was raucous with teenagers.

"Okay," Fran said finally. "I'll deal with her."

Macklin smiled and put out his hand. Fran shook it slowly.

"I'll be in touch," Macklin said.

surveillance was easy enough. Stay out of sight and watch. He'd done a lot of it in L.A. and the greatest enemy was boredom. Tonight in the Back Bay, outside Jenn's apartment, there was no boredom. He'd found space to park on a hydrant in view of her front door. And he sat in his car in the dark with a feeling of such complex intensity that he didn't understand it. He knew that he felt anticipation and anger and excitement, which was at least partly sexual. He also felt calmness and curiosity and hope and guilt and something like strength.

Too hard for me, he said to himself and settled back against the car seat. He didn't let the motor run because that was a dead giveaway to surveillance, a car parked with its motor on. He didn't play the radio. He simply sat and waited. People moved along the sidewalk past his parked car. There was money in the Back Bay and the four-story brick town houses along Beacon Street were full of young, well-dressed, good-looking men and women. It was evening and many of them were coming

Robert B. Parker

home from dinner or movies or working late. Dogs were being walked, and elegantly dressed women in high heels were carrying plastic bags to clean up after them.

Dog shit does not respect social status, Jesse thought.

He looked at his watch. Nine-thirty. If she'd left the station by seven and gone to dinner with somebody, she'd be coming home now. Unless she was spending the night somewhere else. He took in some air and let it out slowly with his lips pursed in a kind of silent whistle.

He felt the comfortable weight of his gun near his right hip. If she were with another guy, he could kill him. He could feel the release it would bring him. He could imagine the near ejaculatory surge of relief he would get, and he rolled the thought around in his mind passionately. And then what. *Now that I've croaked your boyfriend, honey, let's you and me get together?* That wouldn't work. It would also get him jailed. Even police chiefs weren't permitted to kill people for dating their ex-wives. He could probably do it secretively and get away with it. But how many would he have to kill off? And mightn't Jenn get a bit suspicious when her dates kept getting clipped? And how often could he get away with it? Cops normally looked for the disgruntled lover when some men get killed that are dating the same women. He gave it up slowly, knowing he'd never really thought he could. *So why was he here?* He shrugged in the darkness. *Better to know than not know.*

Jenn turned the corner at Dartmouth Street and walked down Beacon Street beside a short man. They were holding hands. Jesse knew Jenn's walk in the dimness before he could recognize any feature. As they got closer, Jesse recognized the evening news anchor, Tony Salt. He was much shorter than he appeared on the tube. Shorter than Jenn. But he had a large head and a strong chin and deep masculine smile lines around his mouth. His walk seemed stilted, and Jesse realized that Tony Salt was teetering on high-heeled cowboy boots. *Christ, in his bare feet he can walk under bar stools,* Jesse thought.

They were walking close together and their shoulders

brushed often. Jenn was talking in that brilliant, animated way she had when she seemed to put her whole self into whatever she was saying. Tony Salt was listening and nodding and laughing often. They walked past Jesse sitting in the darkness and turned into Jenn's doorway. Jesse's concentration was so intense that he didn't realize he had drawn his gun until he clanked it gently against his steering wheel, as he turned in the seat. He rested the gun on the back of the seat, and, knowing he wouldn't shoot, he aimed it carefully at Tony Salt's back and sighted carefully at the spot between Tony Salt's shoulder blades that sat invitingly, and looked a yard wide, on top of the front sight. He held the aim as Jenn fumbled for her keys at the door. Jenn could never find her keys quickly, and when she did find them she never recognized one key from another, so more time ensued while she tried several in the lock before she got the right one. Jesse had always found it endearing that she couldn't find her keys and, indeed, often lost them. Goddesses had no time for keys. Tony Salt stood close to her while she worked on the keys. Jesse knew he was so close that their bodies would be touching every time either of them moved. Jesse could feel how shallow his breathing was. Given the intensity of his feeling, it was surprising that the gun hand was perfectly steady. He squinted a little. He knew it was too far and too dark, but it was as if he could see the weave in the back of Tony Salt's thousand-dollar jacket. Jenn found the right key, and the door opened. She turned and gave Tony Salt a light kiss and stepped through the door. He followed her. With the door still open, they stopped in the lighted hallway and turned the easy kiss into a long embrace, Jenn slouching a little so that she wouldn't have to actually bend down to kiss Tony Salt. Jesse could see Tony Salt's hand move down to Jenn's butt. He had on a big ring that caught the hall light and flashed like Elliott Krueger's ring.

Then they broke the clinch.

The door shut.

"Bang," Jesse said.

chapter 21

"You're the last piece," Macklin said to Freddie Costa.

They were sitting in Macklin's Mercedes in the parking lot near the wharf office on the town pier in Mattapoisett, about ninety minutes south of Boston.

"You need a Northshore guy," Costa said. "Knows the waters. I never even been up there."

"I don't have a Northshore guy," Macklin said. "You didn't know the waters in the Mekong, did you? Besides you're the best sailor I know who's dishonest."

"Thanks," Costa said. "Then if I'm gonna do it, I gotta have time to go up there, cruise around, look at charts. Not only around Paradise but all over that part of the coast."

"Sure," Macklin said. "That's why I'm talking to you early, give you time to plan."

"It'll cost money," Costa said.

"You got to spend money to make money," Macklin said.

"I gotta buy fuel. I got boat payments. I gotta leave my ex with some."

"Haven't you got anything ahead?"

Costa laughed.

"You talking to me about ahead?"

Macklin shrugged. "Okay," he said. "I haven't got too much ahead myself."

"Can't help you without something up-front," Costa said.

Macklin was silent. The harbor around the pier was mostly small sailboats. Some were at their moorings. Their masts bare, the boats tugging gently at the tether. Some were under sail, the mooring marked by the small boat they had rowed out to it. Two kids were fishing off the end of one of the two stone piers. A big old Chris-Craft with gleaming mahogany trim was refueling in the slip between the piers.

"Whatta they catching?" Macklin said.

"The kids? Scup if they're lucky. Blowfish, mostly."

"They good to eat?"

"Scup is, but not the blowfish. Kids like to haul them in, get them to inflate, and skip them on the water."

"There's a good time," Macklin said.

"You know what kids are like."

"No," Macklin said. "I don't."

They were quiet. A rowboat pulled in to the pebbled beach to their right, and two men got out in knee-deep water and dragged the boat up onto the landing area above high tide. The men left the rowboat there and took the oars.The Chris-Craft finished refueling and began to inch out of the slip.

"Okay," Macklin said finally. "I got five grand I can spot you."

"Cash," Costa said.

"Whaddya think? I'm going to write you a check?"

"I don't like to leave nothing to chance," Costa said.

"I could enter the notation: advance on robbery loot," Macklin said.

"You got it on you?"

"No."

"When do I get it?"

"You drive the boat up . . ." Macklin said. Costa began shaking his head before Macklin finished his sentence. "And I'll pay you when you get there."

"Me and the boat stay right here," Costa said. "Until I get the five."

Macklin had known Costa a long time. He was just as he looked. He was squat and strong with thick hands and dark skin that had cured darker in a lifetime on the water, and he didn't change his mind. Once his mind was set, he plowed right through anything in his way—including the law. Costa wasn't scared of Macklin. Costa probably wasn't even scared of Crow. You had the choice of his way or kill him, and Macklin wasn't prepared to kill him yet.

"I'll be here Monday noon," Macklin said.

"With the cash?"

"With the cash."

"Good," Costa said.

"When can you get up there?"

"To Paradise?"

"Yeah."

"You gimme the cash Monday noon, I'll leave Tuesday morning. Go through the canal."

"Good," Macklin said.

Costa nodded. He got out of the car and closed the door. Macklin put the Mercedes in gear, backed up, U-turned, and drove away. In the rearview mirror he could see that Costa hadn't moved.

chapter 22

Copley Place was a high-end, upscale, vertical mall in the middle of Boston. It looked like every other high-end, upscale, vertical mall Jesse had ever seen. When you were in Copley Place, Jesse thought, you could be any-where in western civilization. He had been in Copley Place for three hours, trailing behind Jenn, carrying bags, feeling like a husband, and rather liking it. But he knew he would have to tell her the secret thing he had done, and he was afraid. Usually Jesse could put the fear away, know it was there, but function around it. This fear nearly para-lyzed him.

"You must be making the big buck," Jesse said.

They were sitting beside the waterfall near the top of the escalator in the middle of the second floor.

"I get a clothing allowance," Jenn said. "And I haven't spent it all yet. Are you bored?"

"No," Jesse said. "I like to be with you."

Jenn smiled. But the smile was automatic, Jesse

thought. She was looking at the display in a window down the mall.

"What do you think of that little suit?" Jenn said, "With the chalk stripe."

"It would look good on you." Jesse took a breath. "I followed you the other night when you were out with Tony Salt."

Jenn kept looking at the chalk-striped suit for a moment, and then slowly she turned her head toward him.

"You followed us?"

"Actually I staked out your apartment. I saw you come home with him. I saw him go in."

"And?"

"He spent the night."

Jenn sat back against the bench and kept looking at him.

"Jesse," she said finally, "how . . . how goddamn dare you?"

Jesse clenched himself and held tight.

"I don't know," Jesse said. "I'm ashamed of it."

His voice was steady. Jenn continued to look at him. A woman brought her two small children to the waterfall and let them throw pennies in it. Then she moved on. The kids didn't want to leave. There was an argument. The kids cried. The woman finally dragged them away.

"You . . . have . . . the . . . right," Jesse said slowly, "to . . . date who . . . you wish and . . . spend the night with . . . who you wish."

"Yes," Jenn said. "I do."

"I don't know why I did that," Jesse said.

"I don't know why you're telling me," Jenn said.

"Because it's the truth."

"Do I have to know all the truth?"

"I don't know," Jesse said, "but I have to tell you all the truth."

Jenn smiled. "Well, at least you know it's about you and not about me," she said.

Jesse stared at the artificial waterfall cascading discreetly into the artificial pool.

"I won't do it again," Jesse said.

Jenn could see the way his jaw muscles bunched at the hinges.

"Tell the truth?"

Jesse shook his head.

"I have to do that," he said. "I won't spy on you again."

"Why do you have to tell me the truth, even if it's a bad truth?"

Jesse shook his head as if to clear it. Jenn remembered his doggedness. It was a good quality sometimes, she thought, but not always.

Jenn asked again. "Where does it say you have to always tell me the truth?"

"No secrets," Jesse said.

His voice sounded as if it were being forced through too narrow an opening. God, this is hard on him, Jenn thought. She leaned over and patted his forearm.

"It's hard, Jesse," she said. "You're fighting the booze, you're fighting this. It's hard."

"I don't win this fight, I may not win the booze fight," Jesse said and wished he hadn't as soon as he heard it.

"I know, but I can't help you with that," Jenn said. "I can't be with you so that you won't drink."

"It was the wrong thing to say. Following you was the wrong thing to do." Jesse laughed angrily. "I'm on a roll."

"It's not that bad," Jenn said.

"It was the wrong thing to do," Jesse said.

"Of course it was, but it hasn't changed anything. I'm not going to give up on this because you once acted like a jerk."

Jesse nodded.

"You don't act like a jerk too often anymore," Jenn said.

Jesse grinned at her without any happiness in the grin.

"I'm not sure I like the 'anymore' part," he said.

"How about, you never act like a jerk when you're working," Jenn said.

Jesse nodded. "It's why I work," he said.

chapter 23

When Macklin came in the front door, Faye jumped into his arms and wrapped her legs around his waist. She was wearing a silk robe and nothing else.

"Whoa," Macklin said. "Let me at least get the door closed."

He held her easily.

With her face a half inch from his Faye said, "Welcome home. Wanna fuck?"

"Well, yes," Macklin said, "as a matter of fact I do."

She pressed her mouth against his and held it there while he carried her to the bedroom and put her on the bed. She held on even after he put her down.

"Faye," he said as he pulled away from her. "I need to get my clothes off."

"Well, be quick about it," Faye said as she untied her robe.

She was very inventive and experimental. She liked to try different positions. Whenever she heard of a new sexual trick or an innovative device, she was eager to try it.

There was something joyous in her sexuality. Macklin always thought of her as laughing while they had sex, though he knew she didn't really. When they were through, they lay together on her bed and stared at their reflection in the mirrored ceiling.

"That calm you down for a while?" Macklin said.

"For a while," Faye said. "You hungry?"

"For crissake, Faye," Macklin said. "One appetite at a time. Let me sort of rest up."

"I've got supper ready whenever you want it."

"You serve a nice hors d'ouevre," Macklin said.

"You get the people you want?"

"Yeah, Crow was the most important one. Now I got JD for wiring, and Fran for explosives, and Freddie Costa for the boat."

"That means a five-way split," Faye said.

"Unless some of them drop out," Macklin said.

Faye met his eyes in the mirrored ceiling.

"You think that could happen?"

Macklin smiled and shrugged at her. "Could," he said.

Still looking at him in the ceiling, Faye said, "You're a heartless bastard, Jimmy."

"Not all the time," Macklin said and patted her thigh.

"No," Faye said. "Not all the time."

She put her head against his shoulder, and they were quiet together. Faye knew that it wasn't quite right, what he'd said about "not all the time." He loved her, within his limits, but Jimmy wasn't capable of a lot of feeling. What he could feel most sharply, she knew, was excitement and boredom, and his life was mostly seeking one to avoid the other. It was why jail was so hard on him. She knew that she didn't know what he did to fight boredom in jail, but she knew Jimmy and what excited him was risk. She knew that the odds were good that he'd risk too much someday. And, she knew that he would be unfaithful. It had nothing in his emotional world to do with loving her or not. It had to do with opportunity and conquest. She hated knowing it, but she was a woman who had learned early in life that things were so whether she wanted them to be so or not.

And she knew that she loved him and that he would never leave her, and she would take what there was and make as much of it as she could. Looking up at the two of them lying naked on her bed, Faye thought that probably that was what life was, taking what you could get and making the most of it.

"What's for supper?" Macklin said.

"Pork and pepper stew," Faye said. "And I made a big pitcher of sangria."

"Faye," Macklin said, "you're the best."

Faye knew he meant it, even if he couldn't say she was the only.

"Yes," Faye said. "I am."

chapter 24

Jesse's office was crowded. He was there at his desk. And seated to his right was Nick Petrocelli, the new town counsel. In front of them, in a broad semicircle, were the two Hopkins boys, their father, Charles, their mother, Kay, and their lawyer, Brendan Fogarty. Beyond them was Carleton Jencks, Sr., Carleton Jencks, Jr., known as Snapper, and the Jencks lawyer, Abby Taylor. Earl gave Jesse the finger while pretending to scratch his upper lip. He and Robbie both smirked. Snapper was expressionless.

"As you know, Stone," Fogarty said, "and, as I warned you, the District Attorney's Office has decided that your case against these lads is so tainted by the way you treated them that they won't bring it to trial."

Jesse was motionless, his swivel chair tipped back, while he looked at Fogarty the way he had learned to look at gangbangers in South Central. The stone-faced stare that every big city cop masters his first month in a black and white. To his right Petrocelli was equally motionless, looking bored, staring out the side window at the late gathering evening. He was a dark, slim young guy who wore glasses with big, thick black frames. Jesse wasn't sure about him. Petrocelli had graduated from Harvard Law not very long ago and put in time as a prosecutor in Suffolk County, before he joined a big Boston firm as a litigator. He had moved to Paradise after that and become *pro bono* town counsel when Abby Taylor resigned. But he wasn't thirty yet, Jesse was pretty sure. There was about him a hint of Ivy League condescension, and in the few times Jesse had been with him, he seemed bored in his duties. Fogarty, Jesse noticed, responded to Petrocelli with inadequately concealed amusement. Even Abby, who, except in certain areas that Jesse knew of, was the essence of propriety, seemed heedless of Petrocelli. On the other hand, Jesse thought, the price is right.

"And," Fogarty went on, "it is that same precipitous treatment of these boys that has brought us here tonight. We intend to bring suit, for false arrest and imprisonment."

Jesse turned his stare from Fogarty for a moment and looked at Abby Taylor. She nodded.

"We are part of the suit, Jesse," she said.

Jesse didn't speak. His stare rested heavily once again on Fogarty.

"Do you have anything to say?" Fogarty asked.

Jesse glanced over at Petrocelli.

"Nick?"

"It's America, Jesse, say whatever you want."

Jesse nodded as if that were sage advice. He kept nodding slightly as he looked carefully at each of the people seated in front of him.

"What are you all doing here?" Jesse said.

"I told you," Fogarty began.

Jesse interrupted, "Nobody had to come here for that. You could have sent me a notice in the mail," Jesse said. "Why are you here?"

"Well," Kay Hopkins said. "I can tell you why I'm here."

Her husband said, "Kay . . ."

"Don't you shush me, Charles," Kay bore on. "I wanted to look right into the eyes of the kind of man who would mistreat two little kids."

"Mistreat?" Jesse said.

"Arrested falsely, imprisoned falsely, frightened to death? What would you call it?"

"You guys frightened?" Jesse said to the Hopkins brothers.

"Oh sure," Earl said. "We was scared to death, wasn't we, Robbie?"

"Scared to death," Robbie said and giggled slightly.

Jesse nodded and looked at their mother.

"Don't you talk to them," she said.

"You don't want them talked to, what'd you bring them for?"

"I wanted them to learn that the system does work. That they have parents who will stand up to it and make it work. That police brutality is unacceptable."

"You feel the same way?" Jesse said to Charles Hopkins.

"I feel my sons were badly treated," Hopkins said. "I want to see justice done."

"How 'bout you, Jencks?"

"I haven't decided what I'm here for yet," Jencks said. "I'm listening."

Jesse leaned back in his chair a little farther. Petrocelli seemed almost asleep. He had one elbow on the edge of Jesse's desk and was resting his chin on his fist. He didn't appear to be looking at anything. Jesse surveyed the parents. Charles Hopkins wore a good suit and tie. He was a slim unathletic-looking man, who parted his hair low on the left side and swooped it up over his bald spot. His wife was just overweight enough to make her chic business suit ride a little at the hips. She had a lot of blond hair and considerable eye shadow and a hard mouth. Snapper's father was a big man with square hands and a crew cut. His neck was thick. He wore desert boots and khaki pants and a white short-sleeved dress shirt open at the neck. His forearms were muscular.

"So what have you guys learned so far?" Jesse said.

"That you can't push us around and get away with it," Earl said.

"That's what I learned too," Robbie said.

Jesse looked at the parents.

"Good enough?" he said.

"No," Kay Hopkins said. "I demand that you apologize to these boys."

"Mrs. Hopkins," Fogarty said and put a hand out as if to keep her at bay.

"We hired you, Fogarty," Kay Hopkins said. "You didn't hire us. I'll talk when I want to talk."

"Mrs. Hopkins, as your attorney . . ."

"Oh be quiet. Stone, are you ready to apologize?"

"I'm ready to talk," Jesse said. "As soon as it's my turn."

"I'd like to hear him," Carleton Jencks said.

His voice was deep, and there was authority in it.

"Anyone else got anything else to say?" Jesse said. "I don't want to cut you off."

He looked over the group. No one else spoke. Outside the office windows, it was dark.

"Okay, here's what I know. I know that there were two perfectly nice guys living a perfectly nice life in a perfectly nice house, and these three kids burned it down for the hell of it."

"You can't prove that," Kay said.

"Didn't say I could," Jesse answered. "Said I know it. Robbie told me."

Jesse reached across his desk and punched up the tape recorder.

"No." It was clearly Robbie's voice. *"No. I wasn't even in the house. I was outside watching chickie for the cops."*

"Oh? So who set the fire?" Jesse's voice sounded calm.

"I don't know. I wasn't even in there. Earl had the gas can."

"You're trying to tell me that he was in there with Snapper?"

"Snapper told us he found an open window at the fag

*house and he'd been in there and tagged the walls in the
living room. Earl stole the gas from my dad, for the power
mower, and him and Snapper told me to watch for the
cops, and they went in the house."*

"Through the window?"

"No, Snapper left the door unlocked."

"And you went in and torched the place."

"No." The sound of panic in Robbie's voice was
oppressive in the crowded room. *"No, I didn't. Snapper
and Earl torched it."*

Jesse reached over and shut off the tape recorder.

"Fucking squealer," Snapper said.

"He's lying," Earl said. "Brat."

Carleton Jencks put a hand on his son's knee.

"We're here to listen, son," his voice rumbled softly.
"Not to talk."

"That's not admissible evidence," Kay Hopkins said.
"You intimidated him into saying it."

"Kay," Fogarty said.

"Shut up," Kay said.

"You weren't in the house?" Jesse said to Earl.

"No."

Jesse sighed and ran the tape fast forward and punched
PLAY.

"Snapper made me do it." Earl's voice said. It was
shaky as if he'd been crying. *"We went in the house just to
look around and then we got in there, and Snapper made
me help him."*

"Stop it," Kay Hopkins said. "Stop the tape."

Jesse punched STOP. Kay Hopkins was pale, and there
was a small tremor in her shoulders. Beside Jesse, Nick
Petrocelli had his feet up on the windowsill. His eyes were
closed.

"I didn't say that," Earl said.

"You did too, liar," Robbie said.

"You're the liar," Earl said.

Kay Hopkins turned and slapped the son that was nearest. It was Earl. His eyes filled and his face reddened.

"Kay," her husband said.

"You bastards," she said to her sons, "see what you make me do? Do you like seeing me like this?"

"For God's sake, Kay," Fogarty almost shouted, "will you shut the hell up."

She spun toward him in her chair as if she might slap him too. Her husband stood and put his hands on her shoulders. Jesse hoped she didn't have a weapon.

"Mrs. Hopkins," Jesse said. "You either get yourself under control, or I'll arrest you for assault on a minor child."

Kay didn't look at him. She shook her shoulders, trying to dislodge her husband's hands, and looked at Abby Taylor.

"Well, goddamn it, what about you? You're a woman."

"I think you should be quiet, Mrs. Hopkins. I think you should let your attorney speak for you. I know Chief Stone. He will do what he says he will do."

Slumped on his spine in the chair by the window, with his feet still on the windowsill, Petrocelli opened his eyes and pushed his glasses up on his nose.

"You've probably guessed, Brendan," he said in a strong New York accent, "what the heart of our defense will be if you bring false arrest charges."

"I don't like to guess, Nick."

"Regardless of the final disposition of the case, these tapes are very clear evidence that Chief Stone and the Paradise Police had reasonable cause to arrest these boys."

"What's that mean?" Kay Hopkins said.

"It means he'll pretty likely get to play these tapes in court," Fogarty said.

"Can he do that?"

"Probably," Fogarty said. "Abby?"

"I concur," Abby Taylor said.

"But they can't try these kids for the crime," Jencks said.

"No," Abby said.

Jencks nodded and looked at Jesse.

"Okay. My son and I are not going to bring any false arrest suit," he said.

Jesse nodded. Jencks looked at his son.

"You work too hard at being a tough guy," he said. "We'll talk about that at home."

"You're a tough guy," Snapper said.

"Maybe too tough," Jencks said. "We'll talk about that too."

He stood up.

"We're free to go?"

Jesse nodded again. Jencks took hold of his son's arm and stood him up from the chair. Snapper didn't resist. His father's hand seemed to make him still.

"Come on, Snap," Jencks said, and they walked from the room without looking at Kay or Charles Hopkins as they went.

"I don't know why you hang out with a boy like that. No mother, father working all the time. No wonder he gets in trouble."

"Mrs. Hopkins," Jesse said. "Snapper's got problems, but he's a stand-up kid. He didn't blame either of your sons, and when he heard them blaming him, he didn't deny it."

"So?"

"So your own two kids are a mess. They're criminals. They burned down a couple's house because the couple was gay, if they even know what it means. Neither would accept any blame. They blamed Snapper. They blamed each other. Not much honor there, not much loyalty. No pride at all."

"Don't you lecture me about my children," Kay said.

"Lecture's over. But here's a warning. Every day one of us will look at them. We catch them breaking the law, we will do our best to get them the maximum punishment allowed."

"And I'll have you for harassing them."

"Put that energy into getting them some help, ma'am."

Everyone was quiet for a moment. Then Petrocelli spoke again.

"So," he said, "you bringing suit or no."

Fogarty looked at his clients. "Your call," he said.

Kay Hopkins said, "Well, you're the damned lawyer, Brendan, what do we pay you for?"

"I pay him," Charles Hopkins said. "No, we won't bring suit."

"Then I see no reason to linger," Fogarty said and stood up. "You need a ride, Abby?"

"No, I'll stay and talk with Nick and Chief Stone for a minute," she said.

"Okay."

Fogarty looked at his clients.

"We should go," he said.

Charles and Kay Hopkins and their sons stood and walked out without a word. Fogarty nodded at Petrocelli, and at Jesse, and went out after them and closed the door.

chapter 25

"We need more walking-around money," Macklin said.

"How much you figure?" Crow said.

"Got a lot of mouths to feed," Macklin said, "including yours. Still got some preparation time. I figure maybe twenty, twenty-five would do it."

"You got any thoughts?" Crow said.

"Nope. You're the force guy—go force us some money."

When Crow smiled, deep vertical lines indented on each side of his mouth. "Small bills?" Crow said.

"Be nice," Macklin said.

"See what I can do," Crow said.

When Crow was gone, Macklin went into the kitchen and had coffee and raspberry pie with Faye.

"Think he'll come up with the money?" Faye said.

"Yeah. Crow's the best."

"I thought you were the best, Jimmy."

"Well, yeah, I am, but Crow thinks he's some kind of fucking Apache warrior, you know?"

"Is he Apache?"

"Hell," Macklin said, "I don't know. Says he is."

"I don't like him," Faye said.

"Faye, nobody fucking likes Crow. But he's good at his work and he keeps his word."

"Has he got anybody?" Faye said.

"You mean like a wife or a girlfriend?"

"Yes."

"I don't know," Macklin said. "I don't know anything about Crow, except what he can do."

"Which is kill people?"

Macklin nodded.

"He can kill you with his hands, with a gun, with a knife, with an axe, with a stick, with a length of rope, a sock full of sand, a brick. He can kick you to death. He can drop you from fifty feet with a knife, fifty yards with a hand gun, five hundred with a rifle. He can shoot a bow and arrow. He can probably throw a spear."

"Does he like it?" Faye said.

"He doesn't mind it," Macklin said.

"Neither do you."

"That's right, but he's not like me. He's . . . I've seen guys that like it. I seen guys come off when they kill somebody. He's not like them, either. It's that warrior thing. It's like this is what he does because that's who he is, you know?"

Macklin cut another piece of pie and slid it onto his plate. Faye poured more coffee into his cup.

"You scared of him?" she said.

Macklin looked startled.

"Me? No. You know me, Faye, I don't give enough of a shit to be scared of anything."

Faye smiled and nodded. She had only eaten a bite of her pie.

"What do you give a shit about, Jimmy? I've known you since I was a kid, and I'm not sure if there's anything."

"You, Faye. You gonna eat the rest of that pie?"

Faye shook her head, and Macklin slid her plate over in front of him.

"You do," she said. "Don't you."

"Care about you?"

"Yes."

"I don't care about much else."

"Money," Faye said.

"Oh yeah," Macklin said.

"Actually that's not even exactly right," Faye said. She sipped a little coffee and held the cup up in front of her face with both hands, looking at Macklin over the rim. "It's not quite the money."

"Money's good," Macklin said. "We got any cheese?"

"Refrigerator," Faye said. "In the door thing."

Macklin got up and got the cheese from the compartment in the door of Faye's refrigerator.

"What you really like is stealing it," Faye said.

"If I had to earn it, we'd be poor," Macklin said.

"I doubt it, but that's not the point. You don't want to earn it. You love this — planning, putting together a crew, drawing maps, buying guns, stealing money to keep us going. You like this better than anything."

"No," Macklin said. "I like you better than anything."

"If I asked you to give this up, would you?"

Macklin put down his fork and sat quietly for a moment while he thought about that.

Then he said, "Yes."

Faye sat quietly for longer than he had.

Then she said, "Well, I won't ask you to."

chapter 26

"Very cute," Abby said when they were alone. "How'd you know she'd be a jerk?"

"Given their kids, you had a pretty good shot that one of them was a jerk," Jesse said.

"Even if she weren't, we'd have found occasion to play the tapes," Petrocelli said. "Once they heard them, they weren't going to press the suit."

"What do you think about the kids?" Abby said.

"Snapper maybe has a chance," Jesse said. "Canton and Brown still thinking about a civil suit?"

"Yes, thanks for the business," Abby said. "I referred them to a woman I know at Cone, Oakes."

Petrocelli took his feet down and swiveled his chair around slowly with feet off the ground. He came to rest with his chair tilted back as far as it would go and his toes just touching, in nearly perfect balance.

"Think they'll go forward?" Petrocelli said, looking straight down his nose at nothing.

"They were pretty mad," Jesse said, "when I talked with them."

"The tapes may get played after all," Petrocelli said. "Who'd you send them to?"

"Woman named Rita Fiore," Abby said.

"Used to be a prosecutor," Petrocelli said. "South Shore?"

"Yes. Norfolk County. You know her?"

"She kicked my ass in a thing about two years ago," Petrocelli said. "She's tougher than Jesse."

"No one's that tough," Abby said.

"You think they might admit the tapes in a civil case?" Jesse said.

"Rules of evidence are a little different," Petrocelli said. "And if anyone can get them in, it's Rita."

They were quiet. No one wanted to leave yet. They lingered like players after a game. Jesse got up and walked to the water cooler and got three small plastic cups from the container. He came back and lined them up on his desk. Then he sat back down, took a bottle of Black Bush out of his drawer, and poured a shot into each cup. He handed one to Abby and one to Petrocelli. All three drank sparingly.

"I know you, Jesse," Abby said.

"So I heard," Petrocelli said.

Abby laughed, her face flushing, and continued.

"You must have known you were in danger of tainting the evidence."

Jesse said, "We're all off the record, I assume."

"Right now we're just three friends sitting around talking," Abby said. "I'm surprised you had to ask."

"I knew they did it, but the way I knew it wouldn't stand up in court. I had to get them to confess."

"And you tricked them into thinking each had tattled on the other," Abby said.

"In school," Petrocelli said, "it's tattling. In police stations, it's ratting."

"It's an old cop trick, and if the kids were older and

smarter they wouldn't have fallen for it. Snapper didn't fall for it now. Next time the Hopkins kids won't."

"And there'll be a next time?" Abby said.

"Unless this was the kind of wakeup call that can help them turn it around."

"You think?" Abby said.

"No."

"And you can't help them," Abby said.

"No."

"He did what he could," Petrocelli said.

"Yes," Abby said. "That's why you did it, isn't it? You knew you probably couldn't get them into court, but if you got a taped confession, you might be able to get the parents' attention."

"I didn't want them to think they could burn down some guys' house and walk away from it," Jesse said.

"There needed to be consequences," Petrocelli said. "He created some."

They all thought about that while they sipped their whisky.

"You're a little more than I thought you were," Abby said. "I thought you were a tough guy with an ex-wife."

Jesse nodded. "Still got the ex-wife," he said.

"And when all that was going on with Jo Jo and the Horsemen last year . . ." She paused in mid-sentence and sipped from her second cup of whisky. "I was scared."

Jesse nodded. The room was quiet. Petrocelli was examining the empty space three feet in front of him.

"There was a lot to be scared of," Jesse said.

"For you, too."

"That's sort of supposed to be part of the job," Jesse said.

Abby looked at Petrocelli. "You ever wonder if he can say more than one sentence at a time?" she said.

"I like brevity in a client," Petrocelli said. "Are you trying to tell him you made a mistake last year?"

"I'm trying to apologize for misjudging him."

Petrocelli smiled and swiveled slightly toward Jesse. "Learned counsel says . . ." Petrocelli began.

"I heard her," Jesse said. He looked at Abby. "No apology required. I am a tough guy with an ex-wife."

"Maybe," Abby said.

And the three of them were quiet again for a while, sipping their whisky together in the bright room before they went home for the night.

chapter 27

Crow sat in the back booth of a storefront Chinese restaurant on Tyler Street with a sleek Asian man who said his name was Bo. Bo was wearing a silver-gray leisure suit and a black silk shirt buttoned to the neck. Leaning against the wall behind the booth was a heavyset Chinese man.

"You Portagie?" Bo said.

"Apache."

Bo looked puzzled.

"Indian," Crow said. "Native American."

"Ah," Bo said. "Whores say to pimp you asking about buy a key. Pimp tell someone, someone tell me."

"That's right," Crow said.

"You mind feel for wire?"

Crow smiled and stood and held his arms from his sides.

The heavyset man stepped forward and patted Crow down. When he was finished, he said something in Chinese.

"You have gun," Bo said.

"Yes."

Bo shrugged.

"No problem," he said. "You have money?"

"Not with me," Crow said.

"How you buy? No money?"

"You got the blow?" Crow said.

Bo smiled.

"No with me," he said.

"How you sell, no blow?" Crow said.

Bo shrugged.

"Why you come?"

"Thought I'd look at the product," Crow said. "I like it, we'll arrange something with money."

"You look see blow?"

"Uh-huh."

"You give gun to Vong," Bo said.

"Sure," Crow said.

He took the 9-mm Glock off his hip and handed it butt-first to Vong. Vong took it and dropped it in his side pocket.

"We go," Bo said.

He went out the front door of the restaurant. Crow followed him, and Vong followed Crow. There was a parking lot next door. Bo walked straight to an old Dodge van with Chinese lettering on the side, and in English, hand painted below the Chinese characters were the words FINE PRODUCE. Bo unlocked the back door, climbed in the van, moved some crates around, and came up with a maroon athletic bag with gray lettering on the sides. He dragged the bag by its shoulder strap to the lip of the van bed and opened it. Inside were several kilos of white powder in transparent plastic bags.

"Lemme try," Crow said.

Bo untwisted the plastic tie that closed one of the bags. Crow tasted it.

"Been stepped on some," he said.

"Sure, but it's good stuff. No cut and . . ." Bo rolled his eyes and pretended to fall over.

"Yeah."

Crow picked up the plastic tie and closed the bag. Then he half turned and drove his right heel into Vong's groin. As Vong bent over, he put both hands on Vong's head and snapped his neck with one twist. Crow moved so quickly that Bo was only half out of the truck when Crow got a handful of his hair and yanked him all the way out and slammed his head against the car bumper. He let go of Bo's hair and Bo fell face down on the asphalt. Without any hurry, Crow went to Vong's body and took his Glock out of Vong's pocket. He shot Vong between the already lifeless eyes, and then turned and put one bullet into the base of Bo's skull. Then he put the cocaine back in the bag, zipped it up, picked up the bag, and walked out of the parking lot. There was an attendant in the booth, a thin black man with Rastafarian hair. He was crouching down, trying to hide. Crow walked to the booth and shot him in the head. Then he put his gun back in his holster and walked off down Tyler Street toward Kneeland Street, carrying the maroon Nike bag over his shoulder.

chapter 28

Jesse stood off-camera on the news set at Channel 3 and watched Jenn expertly describing isobars and cold fronts and other things about which he knew she had no clue. She made confident sweeping hand gestures against an empty blue background. Jesse knew that somewhere between Jenn and the television audience the empty blue background acquired a weather map, though he didn't know how. Nor did he care.

The floor director counted her down.

Jenn said, "Back to you, Tony."

When Tony Salt, the news anchor, replaced her on the monitors, Jenn came past the cameras with her finger to her lips, stood beside Jesse, and gave him a small bump with her hip. They stood silently until a commercial break, and then Jenn led them out through the heavy door into the corridor.

"Hi," she said.

"A low-pressure area dominating our weather system?" Jesse said.

Jenn smiled.

"They write it. I read it," she said and stood on her tip-toes to kiss him lightly on the lips. "Where shall we eat?"

"Up to you," Jesse said. "I usually have pizza."

"You know what I'd love?" Jenn said. "I'd love to have some fried clams at that little restaurant on the harbor in Paradise."

"The Gray Gull," Jesse said.

"Yes. Do you mind driving all the way back?"

"No, of course not," Jesse said.

"Oh good. Let me get my purse and stuff, I'll be right back. Don't go anywhere."

Like I would, Jesse thought.

He didn't mind driving forty-five minutes back to Paradise. He would be alone with her. Jenn would sit sideways in the seat next to him, tuck her knees under her, and talk. He had always loved to listen to her talk. She didn't even need to be talking to him. When they had been married, he used to enjoy listening to her talk on the car phone to her agent, her manager, casting directors, girlfriends, hairdressers.

"It's not really about telling people the weather," she said, as they went north through the Callahan Tunnel. The rush hour was over and the traffic was light. "It's about marketing the weather person as a way to market the station," she said. "Otherwise the anchor could just tell you it was going to rain tomorrow as part of the newscast. But that's not the point. There's three of us, for Christ's sake. Clark does noon and eleven. I do six, and Dinah does weekends. I visit schools and street fairs and do remotes from somebody's lobby. That's why I only do six, so they can market me."

"Long day for Clark?" Jesse said.

Jenn nodded.

"He loves it," she said. "Gives him more air time."

"So why you?"

"I got a better ass than Clark."

"I think that's right," Jesse said. "How about Dinah?"

Jenn shrugged.

"Girls with bad asses don't get hired."

Jesse wasn't looking at her. He was watching the road in front of him.

"But she is the weekend weather girl, isn't she," Jenn said.

And Jesse knew without looking just the way her eyes gleamed when she said it.

Jesse took a deep breath and let it out audibly.

"How's Tony Salt," he said. "Is it serious?"

"Not yet."

Jesse felt the thickness in his chest. It began near the solar plexus and reached the lower part of his throat.

"I don't know, Jesse. I'm just dating. It's not serious like you and me, if that's bothering you."

"Could it get that serious?"

"I don't know. I can't promise. I have to be able to see who I want to see, and tonight I want to see you."

"I haven't spied on you again."

"Good."

Jenn didn't say anything, though he was aware that she shifted in the seat so she could look at him more directly.

"I'm ashamed of it," Jesse said.

Jenn nodded. "Knowledge is power," she said.

"That's exactly the phrase my friend used when I told her."

"Your friend's had psychotherapy," Jenn said. "It's a shrink thing to say. This the lawyer lady?"

"No. It's a woman named Marcy Campbell. She sells real estate."

"You fucking her?"

"Yes."

"How come?"

"Well, hell, Jenn, adults fuck, you know?"

"Yep, I know. You love her?"

"No. I like her. I like her a lot. But I don't love her or her me."

Jenn didn't say anything. Jesse drove a quarter way around Bell Circle and headed north past the dog track.

"You think you'll stake me out again?" Jenn said.

"No. You have my word."

"It's a human thing to do, Jesse."

"But not a useful thing," Jesse said.

"No. I have to live my life and see who I wish to see and go where I wish to go and not be trapped in a single commitment."

"Forever?"

"No, just until I don't have to."

"You know when that will be?"

"No. And pushing me on it is counterproductive."

"I know."

"I can't make you promises, Jesse. I can't give you any guarantees. It scares me even to talk this much about it. But you have to remember that you and I are connected in a way that I've never been connected to anyone else."

"You love me?"

"Yes."

"That's a good basis," Jesse said.

"Yes, it is. I think it is possible to love other people too. I think people can love more than one person. On the other hand, so far, I haven't."

"That's encouraging too."

"I want to encourage you as much as I can, Jesse. I don't want to lose you."

"You won't lose me," Jesse said.

chapter 29

Mrs. Campbell was wearing a tailored brown suit with a vertical blue stripe. *It was tight on her but tight in a good way,* Macklin thought. It didn't look like it was too small; it just fit her close.

"Just wanted to be sure it would be okay to bring a couple of guys over. My contractor and maybe one of his people?"

"Of course, Mr. Smith," Mrs. Campbell said.

"Harry."

Mrs. Campbell smiled. "People do it all the time, Harry. We realize it's a large investment, and we encourage them to take their time, make sure they're happy. Satisfied customers are our best marketing tool."

"I'll bet most of your customers are satisfied," Macklin said.

Mrs. Campbell met his look. Her face looked a little flushed to him. He could smell her. Soap, shampoo, perfume.

"Most," she said.

"May I call you Marcy?" Macklin said.

"Please."

"Marcy, I'd like to try the restaurant on the island, and I hate to eat alone. You free for lunch?"

"As a bird," Marcy said.

The restaurant was called Stiles'. They got a table by the big picture window and ordered drinks. Looking out at the ocean, Macklin could see what Freddie had meant. The sea burst in upon a random scatter of rust-colored boulders that littered the coast of the island in both directions. The water among the boulders was creamy with foam.

Marcy had a glass of white wine. Macklin ordered a martini.

"Be tough sailing off this side of the island," Macklin said.

"Certainly would be," Marcy said. "It's why the docking facilities are on the harbor side."

"Do any sailing?" Macklin said.

"No." Marcy smiled. "I'm a dry land girl, I'm afraid."

"Indoor sports, so to speak," Macklin said.

Again Marcy met his look. Her face still had a lot of color to it. Maybe she was just naturally high colored. And maybe he was going to get her. More than maybe. Faye would understand. Marcy Campbell would be useful. He'd understand if it were the other way.

"So to speak," Marcy said.

They both smiled. The spray from the turmoil below them spattered up sporadically against the stained glass. The dark paneled dining room was nearly empty, and the people that were there spoke quietly.

"What's your husband do, Marcy?" Macklin said.

"Ex-husband," Marcy said.

"Ah," Macklin said.

"Ah, indeed," Marcy said. "How about yourself— how'd you make your money?"

"Liquor stores, mostly," Macklin said. "Couple banks."

"Always interests me," Marcy said, "how some people

have a knack for making money and others don't. What's
your secret?"

"Mostly it's not caring if you do or don't," Macklin said.
"Mostly you just got to enjoy the game. How about you—
you enjoy real estate?"

"Get to meet some interesting people," Marcy said. "I
like interesting people."

"And you enjoy the game?"

"Very much," Marcy said.

They ordered lunch. *Yeah,* Macklin thought, *I've got
her.* It was business, but that didn't prevent him from getting that nice ratchety feeling he always got as he circled in
on a woman he'd never slept with. Faye was always curi-
ous. *How did you know? How can you tell?* He watched
Marcy as they ate lunch. When he told Faye about it, she'd
want to know. *What did you talk about? How did she act?*

After lunch they went back to the real estate office.
When they went in, Macklin could feel the tension. They
were alone together in a private place. Marcy turned and
looked at him. He was silent, looking back at her. He knew
it would happen. He could feel it spread through him.

"What game are we playing now?" Marcy said.

"I'm not sure," Macklin said. "But I'm enjoying the hell
out of it. You want to go someplace?"

Marcy walked over to the front door and turned the
lock. Then she went to the little picture window and
closed the venetian blinds.

"No need to go someplace," Marcy said and sat down
on the couch, patting the cushion beside her.

"No need at all," Macklin said.

It had been a smart move to leave his gun in the car. He
sat beside her.

"You knew when you came in here, didn't you?" Marcy
said.

"Uh-huh."

"How?"

"Something about you," Macklin said, "I can always
tell."

"Me too," Marcy said.

"With men, it's easy," Macklin said.

"Good point."

Naked beneath him on the couch, Marcy thought how much stronger he was than he looked with his clothes on. Like Jesse was. Above her, Macklin thought that she wasn't better than Faye, but she was nearly as good. Like Faye, she moved a lot and was noisy. Nothing beats enthusiasm in a woman, Macklin thought. He loved Faye. But this hadn't anything to do with Faye. It didn't mean anything to him, and he knew it didn't mean anything to Marcy. She was like him. She liked a good time. And then he let himself go and didn't think about much of anything for a little while.

chapter 30

It was nearly 7:30 and the sun was down when they settled in at the bar in the Gray Gull.

"I'd like a martini," Jenn said. "Up, extra olives."

"You got it," Doc said. "Jesse?"

"Black label and soda," Jesse said. "Tall."

Doc put the drinks in front of them and put out a hand to Jenn.

"I'm Doc," he said.

"Oops," Jesse said. "Sorry, this is my, this is Jenn."

"Hi, Doc."

"Hello, Jenn."

It was almost fall, and the summer crowd had mostly left. There were several empty tables and four or five stools available at the bar. By 9:00, the place was nearly full. Jesse was trying to nurse his scotch.

"Do you have to get up early?" Jenn said.

"I should be at the station by nine," Jesse said. "But I always get up early. Seven is sleeping in for me."

"Why do you get up so early?" Jenn said. "You didn't used to."

"Don't sleep well," Jesse said.

"Well, I think we should go," Jenn said.

"Okay."

Jesse paid the bar bill, left twenty percent for Doc, and walked out behind Jenn. Several people recognized her and stared covertly.

In the car, Jenn said, "It's a long ride back to Boston, Jesse. I think I should stay with you."

"Okay," Jesse said.

What did "with" mean? He stifled the question. *Let it play out,* he thought.

His condominium was only five minutes from the Gray Gull. Inside, Jenn went straight to the living room and opened the French doors onto the little deck over the water.

"I love this view," she said.

Jesse went and stood beside her on the deck. House lights were scattered brightly against the solid blackness of Paradise Neck. The salt sea smell of the harbor was strong.

"Funny how different this ocean seems," Jenn said.

"Maybe we're different," Jesse said.

"That would be nice."

Jesse felt compressed by the tension between them. He wondered if Jenn even felt it. She seemed perfectly in possession of herself. They were quiet. Jesse stood next to her, not touching her. Except for the sound of the ocean moving below them, the silence was crystalline. *Maybe I can't stand this,* Jesse thought. *Maybe I need a drink.* To his left, the head of the harbor was darkened by Stiles Island where barely any lights showed. *Everything faces the ocean,* Jesse thought. *Got their back to the town.* He didn't look at Jenn, though he felt her next to him the way he felt the pull of gravity.

"Jesse," she said.

He turned. She had turned toward him. Her face was raised to him. Subtly, beneath the heavy ocean smell, he could smell her perfume. He opened his arms, and she pressed against him. He kissed her. She opened her mouth and kissed him back. He was conscious of his breath surging in his lungs, of the blood moving through the intricate riparian patterns of his arteries and veins, the electricity tracing his nerves and muscles. They began to fumble at each other's clothes. Jenn broke away long enough to gasp, "Living room." She pressed her mouth against his again as they stumbled into the living room. They went to the carpet and made love there. It was all visceral. Whatever sounds they made were inarticulate. In the darkness, hours after they had begun, they paused long enough to go into Jesse's bedroom.

Jesse woke up in bright sunshine. He was lying on his back. Jenn was beside him, still asleep, in the crook of his arm, with her head on his chest. He looked at his wrist. His watch wasn't there. He looked over at the alarm clock on the bureau. It was 10:40. He had not slept much past dawn since he'd come east. Actually, as he thought about it, he had not slept past dawn since Jenn started fucking Elliot whatsisname. Maybe he should have killed Elliott. He always regretted that he hadn't. He wasn't sure he could have. He had shot people and maybe he would again. But just walk up and shoot him? Had he done so, he would never be lying here in the mid-morning sunshine, with Jenn naked beside him. He had been right not to . . . but he knew, and he smiled secretly in the still room at the knowledge, that there would always be, in one small compartment of his soul, the regret that he hadn't. The seagulls were loud. The harbor smell was assertive. The French doors were still open.

Without opening her eyes, Jenn said, "Don't make too much of this."

"Okay," Jesse said.

"It doesn't mean we should move in together or start dating each other exclusively or get married or any of those things."

"Right," Jesse said.

"It just means we are fond of each other and maybe love

each other and probably want to date each other again, and we're grown-ups."

"Correct," Jesse said.

Jenn gave him the look. The same look he knew she'd had when she spoke of the other weather woman being on weekends.

"And," Jenn said, "grown-ups fuck."

"Do they ever," Jesse said.

They lay together for a while, her head on his chest, his arm around her shoulder, then Jenn swung her feet off the bed and stood up.

Her hair was messy, and her makeup was smeared. Naked, she walked from the bedroom, following the trail of discarded clothing to the deck.

"Gee," she said. "What possibly could have gone on here?"

"Nothing bad," Jesse said.

"No," Jenn said, "nothing bad."

chapter 31

"Harry Smith," Macklin said when he came into Jesse's office. "Thanks for taking the time."

"Happy to," Jesse said.

He stood while they shook hands. Macklin's grip was stronger than Jesse had expected from a guy who looked like an amateur golfer. Macklin took a chair across the desk from him.

"Here's the deal, chief. I'm thinking about buying property on Stiles Island. I don't need to tell you that I'm looking at a good-sized investment if I do."

"Good-sized," Jesse said.

"So I'm trying to size up the whole town, not just the island."

"Uh-huh."

"You don't mind, do you, me talking to you?"

"I don't mind," Jesse said.

"How's the crime situation?"

"Good," Jesse said.

"You mean, there isn't much," Macklin said.

"A lot of the time, there isn't any."

Macklin smiled.

"So what do you guys do?"

"Write traffic tickets. Keep the kids from loitering. Had a case of arson a while ago."

"Really?" Macklin said. "Jewish lightning?"

"No, teenage kids with a grudge."

"You catch them?"

"Yeah."

"Cops one, teenagers nothing," Macklin said. "Heard you had some trouble year or so ago."

"Yeah, couple of murders."

"Crimes of passion?"

"You could say that."

"You catch the guy?"

"Yeah."

Macklin smiled again.

"Cops two," he said.

Jesse was quiet.

"You got a big force?" Macklin said.

"No. Twelve officers and me."

"Four per shift," Macklin said.

"That's how the math works."

"You been chief long?"

"Long enough," Jesse said.

"Work your way up from the ranks?"

"No."

"Came from another department."

"Yes."

"Where?"

"Elsewhere."

Macklin leaned back a little and studied Jesse.

"You're a pretty quiet guy," Macklin said.

"True."

"Probably the right way to be," Macklin said. "Me, I'm a talker. My wife's always telling me to quiet down."

Jesse didn't say anything. He seemed attentive. Macklin sensed no hostility in him. He was just quiet. There was no way to know what went on behind his eyes.

"How's the security on Stiles?" Macklin said.

"Secure," Jesse said.

"They got their own security force, I see."

"Um-hmm."

"They tied in with you guys?"

"You need to talk to them."

Macklin nodded slowly, as if confirming a long-held assumption. He stood with a wide smile and put out his hand. Jesse shook it.

"I'm encouraged, chief," Macklin said. "You can usually count on a man who doesn't say more than he has to."

Jesse smiled. Macklin smiled back and left.

In the car with Faye, Macklin was silent.

"How'd it go?" Faye said as she drove up Summer Street. "You find out what you wanted to know?"

"I got a read on the chief," Macklin said. "Which is what I wanted, I guess."

Faye slowed the car as they passed a couple of kids on bicycles.

"But?"

"But he's not what I wanted him to be," Macklin said.

Faye braked at the stop sign on Beach Street, looked carefully both ways, and drove on.

"So what is he?"

"I don't know," Macklin said. "But he's not a shit-kicker."

"Well," Faye said, "neither are you."

Macklin patted Faye's thigh for a moment and smiled.

"No," he said. "I'm not."

chapter 32

Tony Marcus was a black man with a big moustache and a small Afro. He had on good clothes, Crow noticed. A dark pinstriped suit, a bright white shirt with a wide spread collar. His pink silk tie was tied in a big Windsor knot.

"Who sold you this crap?" Tony Marcus said.

Crow smiled and shook his head. They were in the back room of a restaurant called Buddy's Fox. Marcus was sitting at his desk. Crow sat across from him. The two men with Marcus were standing. One was a huge man called Junior. The other one was a fidgety, skinny kid with his hair slicked back and a large gold ring in his ear. The kid's name was Ty-Bop. He'd be the shooter, Crow thought.

"Well, whoever it was, they seen you coming."

"It's been stepped on a little," Crow said.

"The sample you gave me's been trampled on," Marcus said.

"So buy it cheap, sell it for double."

"How'd you get to me?" Marcus said.

"I asked around."

"Where'd you get the blow?"

Crow smiled again and said nothing.

"Coke dealer named Bo Chang got clipped the other night in Chinatown. Know anything about that?"

"Nope."

"Where you from?" Marcus said.

"Out of town," Crow said.

"You Mexican or something?"

"Apache," Crow said.

"Apache?"

"Yes."

"Like fucking Geronimo Apache?"

"Yes."

Marcus looked at Ty-Bop.

"You know who Geronimo was, Ty-Bop?"

Ty-Bop shook his head. He was restless. Never quite still, tapping his hands against his thighs, shifting his feet as if he were jiving to a music of his own.

"How about Apache?" Marcus said. "You know about Apaches, Ty-Bop?"

"You know I don't know nothing about that shit, Mr. Marcus."

"That's okay, Ty-Bop," Marcus said. "You know what you need to know."

Ty-Bop nodded. Junior, taking up most of the wall he was leaning on, said nothing.

"What you call cheap?" Marcus said.

"Hundred for the lot."

"Hundred large?" Marcus said.

"Yes."

"Dream on, Geronimo."

"What you call cheap?" Crow said.

"Twenty."

"Apiece?"

Marcus shook his head.

"Twenty grand for the lot?" Crow sounded amazed.

"For crissake," Marcus said. "What I'm buying is about three keys of mannite."

"It's not that bad," Crow said.

"You want to talk to my chemist?" Marcus said. "It's shit. Means I got to market it to white college kids."

"Lot of them in Boston," Crow said.

"Why I'm offering you twenty."

"You got it here?" Crow said.

"Yes."

"Count it out," Crow said. "I'll be right back."

Crow went out through the restaurant to where his car was parked on the street. He opened the trunk of his car, picked up the Nike bag, closed the trunk, and went back in through the restaurant. He put the bag on the desk. Marcus looked in it, sampled a little from each kilo, and shook his head in distaste.

"Yeah, same shit," he said.

He pushed a stack of hundreds across the desk. Crow picked it up and counted it. There were 200 of them.

"Okay," Crow said.

He stuffed the bills into his two side pockets.

"You took kind of a chance, didn't you?" Marcus said. "Come in here alone, selling me stuff. How'd you know we wouldn't just take it away from you?"

"Your reputation," Crow said. "You'd have to kill me to do it, and I figured it wasn't worth it to you for three kilos of baby laxative."

"I guess you figured right," Marcus said.

Crow looked at Ty-Bop, jittering near the door somewhere in his own world.

"And maybe I didn't think you could do it," Crow said.

Marcus grinned. "Don't let Ty-Bop fool you," Marcus said. "He's pretty good."

"I guess we don't need to find out now," Crow said.

"Bo Chang was a tough little fucker," Marcus said.

Crow shrugged and went out of the office.

chapter 33

"Guy named Harry Smith," Jesse said.

"Never heard of him," Suitcase Simpson said.

"Said he's buying property on Stiles Island, told me he wanted to get a feel for the town before he commits."

Suitcase shrugged.

"So. That makes sense. Guy's gonna lay out big bucks, wants to know he's in the right place."

"Maybe."

"What else?"

Suitcase was a big round kid with blond hair and red cheeks. He'd been a tackle on the Paradise High School team. He was ten years younger than Jesse and smarter than you thought he'd be.

"I don't know," Jesse said. "I felt like I was getting hustled."

"What'd he say?"

"He asked about crime and how many policemen we had and how Stiles Island Security tied in with us."

"You think he's going to pull a job, and before he does,

he comes and, like, checks with the chief of police?" Suitcase said.

"Doesn't seem likely, does it?"

"Nope."

Jesse let his swivel chair back and put his feet up on the desk and looked out the window at the desultory traffic on Summer Street.

"When I was working South Central," Jesse said, "some of the gangbangers would see you parked on the street, and they'd come over and talk with you. Buddy-buddy like, couple of cops, couple of robbers passing the time."

"In L.A.?"

"In L.A."

"Why would they do that?" Suitcase said. "I'd figure they hated cops."

"They did, and they didn't," Jesse said. "We were how they knew what they were, if you follow what I'm saying."

"You were what?" Suitcase said.

"They were the other side of us. We were the law tough guys; they were the outlaw tough guys. They kind of flirted with us."

"Flirted?"

"Like a woman," Jesse said, "who wants you to be interested in her, but probably won't go to bed with you."

"Like a cock-teaser," Suitcase said.

"Like that," Jesse said. "Want us to know they were bad. Didn't want us to catch them at it."

"And you're saying Harry Smith is a cock-teaser?"

Jesse grinned. "Talking to him reminds me of talking to those gangbangers."

"He's letting you know he's bad?" Suitcase said.

"He might be," Jesse said.

"Why would he do that?"

"Maybe he likes foreplay," Jesse said.

"Foreplay?"

"Some bad guys are bad guys because they like the action. They get excited by the danger of being a bad guy. And it gets more exciting if you make it more dangerous.

Not getting caught is even more fun if you almost get caught."

"Jesus, Jesse, sometimes you get these theories . . ."

"You know any compulsive gamblers?"

"Every cop knows a compulsive gambler," Suitcase said. "They get in trouble."

"Right, what is it they like about gambling?"

"The action?"

"And what creates the action?"

"I don't know."

"What makes gambling a gamble?" Jesse said.

Suitcase stared at him, concentrating. Jesse waited. Then Suitcase's wide pink face relaxed a little.

"That you might lose."

"That's it. You get it about the gangbangers and Smith?"

"Yeah. If he's that way. I mean, you're the chief, Jesse, and I'm just a patrolman . . ."

"Senior investigative patrolman," Jesse said.

"Yeah, sure, but whatever, but maybe Mr. Smith is just worried about the security of his real estate investment."

"Maybe he is," Jesse said. "Let's see if we can find out."

Jesse handed Suitcase a pink telephone message slip. There were numbers written on the back.

"When Smith left here," Jesse said, "his wife picked him up in a car with those plates on it. Why don't you run them down."

Suitcase took the slip and folded it into his shirt pocket.

"If he's buying real estate on Stiles," Suitcase said, "he must be doing business with one of the brokers."

"Marcy Campbell," Jesse said. "I saw her with him and his wife at the regatta dance."

"You know I never been to one of them?"

"I'll get you a paid detail for the next one," Jesse said. "See what you're missing."

"Want me to talk to Mrs. Campbell too?"

"No, I'll do that."

Suitcase did a small double take.

"Something going on, Jesse?"

Jesse smiled. "What makes you think so?" Jesse said.

"Just something about how you said that so quick," Suitcase said. "You tagging Mrs. Campbell?"

"We're friends, Suit," Jesse said. "I like her."

"Lotta people been friends with Mrs. Campbell."

"Find out about Harry Smith, Suit. I'll talk with Mrs. Campbell."

"Sure, Jesse."

"Ask around a little too. But not too obvious. I'd rather he didn't know we were asking."

"Okay," Suitcase said.

He stood and went to the door.

"You know, I think Abby Taylor's getting interested in you again too," Suitcase said. "She was asking me about you when I was getting coffee at the Village Room."

"What was she asking?"

"About you and your ex, and were you going out with anyone. Stuff like that."

"Just polite conversation," Jesse said.

"No it was not," Suitcase said.

Jesse shrugged. Suitcase was a heavy-handed kidder but an enthusiastic one.

"Man," he said. "Mrs. Campbell, your ex, now Miss Taylor. You're a damn golden boy, Jesse. I wish I was from California."

"I wish you were in California," Jesse said. "Go investigate Harry Smith."

"Yessir, Chief Stone."

chapter 34

Macklin looked around happily. He had the whole crew with him, ranged in a semicircle in Faye's living room. It was the first time he had them all together. Faye served drinks.

"Drink up," Macklin said. "Because when we get close, everybody goes on the wagon."

"How close are we now?" Crow said.

"Still gathering data," Macklin said. "What's the ocean look like around the island, Freddie?"

"Channel between the island and the neck is not navigable. Way the water churns in there, be like navigating a blender."

"So?"

"So if I take you off on this side, at the boat club, which is the only place I can, I got to go all the way around the island to get to the open sea."

"Puts us between the town and the island for how long?"

"Depends on which way the tide is and which way the wind's blowing at the time."

"For crissake, Freddie, gimme a time. Ballpark."

"Half hour."

"Too long. Can you take us off the other side?"

"Long as the weather holds. Take you right off by the restaurant, but you got to get to me. I can't get in closer than maybe fifty yards."

"Too shallow?"

"Too shallow. Too rocky. There's a lot of rock jumble slid down off the stone face over the last million years."

"So how do we get to you?"

"Wade out. It's only about five feet deep at the most. I hold the boat steady out past the rocks. You walk out to me."

Macklin nodded.

"We'll work something out," he said. "Maybe we can find a small rowboat and stash it."

"Either way," Costa said, "weather's got to be good."

"We'll try to pick a nice day," Macklin said.

Costa heard the sarcasm. He paid no attention. He knew what he knew. Bad weather, you couldn't get through those rocks. Couldn't get anything but a small boat through there in any kind of weather. And he wasn't tearing his boat up on those rocks for Macklin or a million bucks or anything else. They didn't know about the ocean. He did.

"Anybody needs to get onto the island, you take my car," Macklin said. "The real estate broad thinks you're my contractors. She gave me a visitor's pass because I'm such a hot prospect. You put the pass on the dashboard and drive up, and the guard waves you through."

"I'll need a look at the underside of the bridge," Fran said.

"Freddie will get you as close as he can, and you can use binoculars," Macklin said. "JD, you go with them. I think all the wire from the island runs under the bridge."

"What makes you think that?" JD said.

"Mrs. Campbell told me."

"Maybe she's just saying it. Sell you some property."

"Well, where else would they run it?"

"On the floor of the harbor."

"When they have a nice bridge?"

"They might have wanted power out there while they were building the bridge."

"Okay," Macklin said. "We won't guess. Find out about it."

"Yessir, cap'n," JD said.

Macklin gestured his glass at Faye, and she made him a new drink and put it at his elbow. She put her hand on his shoulder as she set the drink down. Macklin patted her hand absently.

"Weapons?" Crow said.

Macklin nodded. "Shotguns. Rifles. Hundred rounds each."

Crow raised his eyebrows.

"Better too much than too little," Macklin said. "Everybody here got a piece of his own?"

"I got a Winchester on the boat," Costa said.

"Handgun," JD said.

Fran nodded.

"Crow, make sure each of us has rifle, shotgun, and handgun," Macklin said. "Fran, you'll take care of your own explosives?"

"Soon as I figure out what I need," Fran said.

Faye brought in a platter of sandwiches, mixed some more drinks, leaned her hips against the sideboard, and watched Jimmy when she wasn't busy. He's happy, she thought. He loves this, getting the crew together, planning the action, attending to all the details, smoothing out any friction. He should have been some kind of army officer. She watched him lean back in his chair sipping his drink, a triangular sandwich half in his other hand. *He loves these guys,* Faye thought. It bothered her a little that he'd gone to see the police chief. Jimmy was a thrill seeker. It was why he did what he did. He needed to get too close to the edge. The greater the risk, the greater the excitement. Some times he risked too much. She hadn't liked Jimmy's reaction to the chief. The chief was more than Jimmy had expected.

"How about a bazooka," Macklin was saying.

"A bazooka?" Crow said.

"Rocket launcher, whatever, so if there's a police boat we can blow them out of the water."

"I'll put it on the list," Crow said.

Faye couldn't tell if Crow was smiling or not.

chapter **35**

Jesse met Abby Taylor at the Gray Gull. Abby had a martini. Jesse ordered beer. Abby noticed but said nothing. Jesse smiled and raised his glass toward Abby.

"Old times," he said.

Abby tapped her glass against his.

"Good times," she said.

"Yes."

The bar was crowded. The outside deck was closed for the season, and most of the tables inside were full.

"But I didn't ask you to meet me just for that," Abby said.

Jesse nodded.

"Kay Hopkins is going to try and have you removed as chief," Abby said. "The two gay guys whose house was burned . . ."

"Canton and Brown," Jesse said.

"Yes. They're proceeding with their civil suit, and I imagine the Hopkins will have to settle, because they don't want to get into court and have your tapes played."

"I wouldn't think so," Jesse said.

"But she's not willing to let it go. "

"Mrs. Hopkins."

"Yes. She feels you have misused her darling boys, and then misused your office to suggest a civil suit. She's going to get you."

"If she can," Jesse said.

"She's already talked with Morris Comden. You know Morris."

"Morris is not like a rock," Jesse said.

Doc came down the bar. "Another round?" he said.

Abby nodded. Jesse shrugged. He still had half a beer in front of him. He wasn't about beer. Which was why he was drinking it.

"Talk to Nick Petrocelli about this," Abby said. "Don't take her lightly. She is vicious and driven. She needs to get her own way. And she's not used to being thwarted."

"Beware a woman scorned," Jesse said.

Doc served the second round. Abby had a good pull on her second martini.

"Like me," she said.

Whoops, Jesse thought.

"I thought you scorned me," he said.

"I suppose I did."

"You're not the first," Jesse said.

Abby took one of the olives out of her martini and ate it. "I gather that Jenn is still in town."

"Yes."

"How are you and she doing?"

"I don't know."

"What kind of answer is that?" Abby said.

"The truth," Jesse said. "I don't quite know what our relationship is or how it's going to turn out."

"How would you like it to turn out?"

Jesse drank some of his first beer.

"She says she's not the same person."

Abby took another drink. "So?"

"If that's true . . ."

"You want to be with her," Abby said.

"If I can be."

Abby nodded her head slowly and kept nodding it. "What's she say?" Abby asked.

"She says we're two single adults, and we can date each other and other people and see where it all leads."

"Does she want to be with you?"

"She does and she doesn't," Jesse said.

"What the hell does that mean?" Abby said.

She finished her martini and nodded at Doc.

"It means she wants to be with me, and she doesn't want to be with me," Jesse said. "I think the shrinks call it ambivalence."

"And you're supposed to wait around until she decides?"

"If I want to," Jesse said.

"And you want to?"

Doc brought Abby a fresh drink. He looked at Jesse, who shook his head. Doc went away.

"If I can be with Jenn, I will be," Jesse said carefully.

Abby was silent, slowly twirling the stem of her martini glass on the bar. Jesse was quiet, waiting. Abby's eyes began to tear. Jesse took in some air.

"And what about us?"

"I thought we were history," Jesse said.

"I thought we were too," Abby said. "I was wrong. I was frightened by what happened last year. I was frightened by how hard you were. I didn't understand."

"And now you don't mind? Or now there's nothing frightening going on?"

"Now I understand."

Jesse nodded. Abby was starting to slur her S's.

"There's no reason, in the short run at least, why we can't see each other," Jesse said. "You seeing anyone else?"

"I've been dating Paul Graveline. "

"You like him?"

"Very much."

He remembered how she'd looked naked, how she'd been in bed. He liked the memory. Abby stopped twirling her glass and looked up at him. The tears had spilled from her eyes and were now running down her face.

"But?" Jesse said.

"But . . . I love you, Jesse."

"That's not a good idea, Abby."

"I know."

"I've never pretended," Jesse said. "I've always told you the truth."

"I know. You said, 'Abby, don't put all your eggs in my basket.' "

Jesse nodded. He drank some more beer. He wanted more lift than the beer gave him. Seated alone at a table for two across the room was Harry Smith's wife. Jesse remembered her from the Race Regatta Cotillion where he'd seen her and Harry with Marcy Campbell. She had a nearly full glass of red wine in front of her.

"But I did," Abby said.

Jesse didn't have anything to say.

Mrs. Smith across the room was still at her table alone, her wine glass was still more full than empty. She seemed comfortable drinking alone at the table.

"Even if you were back with Jenn, somehow . . ." Abby said. She paused to finish her martini. "Even if you were, we could still maybe have our little relationship on the side."

"Maybe not," Jesse said. "It's too complicated for me to say yes and no to anything, but maybe we couldn't."

Abby with the tears running down her face, gestured at Doc for another drink. Doc looked at Jesse. Jesse nodded. *Shutting her off now would not be smart,* he thought. Doc brought her the drink and gave Jesse another look. Jesse shrugged. Abby drank half her drink and slid off the bar stool and put her arms around Jesse's neck and kissed him hard. He should stop this now, he thought. But he didn't. Abby finished kissing him and leaned away, her arms still around his neck.

"Tell me you didn't like that," she said.

"I won't tell you that."

"Tell me you don't want me to come home with you."

He should stop this now. "I won't tell you that either," he said.

She pressed in close against him again and kissed him with her mouth open. Jesse always felt he was on display in the town where everyone knew he was the chief of police. Just as he would never allow himself to get drunk in public, he didn't want to be seen necking in public. He was uncomfortable and thick and intense. *This must be ambivalence,* he thought.

With her lips brushing his and her pelvis pressed against him, Abby whispered, "Take me home, Jesse."

"Yes," he said.

They left the Gray Gull with Abby clinging to him. He wasn't sure if it was desire or dizziness. Probably both, he decided.

When they were gone, Mrs. Smith got up and walked to the bar and spoke to Doc.

"The young woman with Chief Stone," Faye said. "She looks so familiar to me. What is her name?"

"Abby Taylor, ma'am."

"She live here in town?"

"Yes ma'am, used to be town counsel."

"I'm sure we've met. You wouldn't know if she went to Wellesley College, would you?"

"No, ma'am."

Faye smiled at him. "Well, no matter," she said. "Next time I see her, I'll ask her."

chapter 36

Macklin sat drinking coffee with Crow in Macklin's car parked outside the Stiles Island branch of the Paradise Savings Bank. An armored car pulled away from the bank.

"Lot of cash in that bank," Macklin said.

"You think?"

"Second armored car delivery of the day," Macklin said. "They are not bringing office supplies."

Crow nodded. He was slouched in the front seat, one foot propped on the dashboard. Even relaxed, Crow carried with him an aura of force barely contained and waiting to explode.

"Another thing to notice," Macklin said, "you going to be a successful bank robber, is how many ATM's they got. "

"They got four," Crow said.

"Nice eye, kemo sabe. And if you look up and down the street here, what do you see?"

"Lotta WASP pussy," Crow said.

"Besides that," Macklin said.

"Places for the WASP pussy to shop."

"Bank robber's tip number two. Find a bank near a lotta retail shops."

"Because?"

"Lotta cash required."

"Ah," Crow said. "How about safe deposit boxes?"

"They got 'em," Macklin said. "I checked."

"Lotta trouble getting into safe deposit vaults."

"Is if you got to bust them. Not so hard if the owners open them up for you."

"Don't you need a bank key too?"

"Sure."

Crow sipped some coffee. He watched a woman in spandex tights get out of a silver Volvo station wagon and walk away from them toward a food shop called the Island Gourmet.

"Jimmy," Crow said thoughtfully, "just how much time you plan spending during the commission of this crime?"

"Coupla days ought to do it."

"And you don't think the cops or nobody might, ah, intervene?"

"Not if they don't know nothing about it," Macklin said.

"And you think you can keep them from knowing?"

"I do."

"For how long?"

"Coupla days, maybe."

"And if they find out sooner?"

"They still got to get out here and stop us."

"You going to blow the bridge?"

"If I need to."

"No way we're going to make this omelette, Jimmy, without breaking a few eggs," Crow said.

"You care?"

"No."

"What the hell do you care about, Crow?"

"Nothing you'd understand, Jimmy."

"Apache stuff?"

Crow shrugged and sipped some more coffee.

"Sure," he said.

"Well we get-um much wampum," Macklin said. "Apaches care about wampum, don't they?"

"Apaches don't know nothing about wampum, that's East Coast Indian shit."

"So what do Apaches care about?"

"Cash," Crow said.

chapter 37

"That registration you wanted me to check?" Suitcase said as he came into the office. "Car's registered to Harry Smith, okay. Address on Pier Seven in Charlestown." He handed Jesse the pink message sheet. Jesse glanced at it. The address was the rehabbed Charlestown Navy Yard. He folded the pink slip and put it in his shirt pocket.

"Heard you was with Abby at the Gull last night," Suitcase Simpson said. "Heard she had a few."

"Observant," Jesse said.

"Heard she was all over you."

"I think one is connected to the other," Jesse said.

"She spend the night at your place?"

"Suit, maybe you should start dating more," Jesse said.

"Me and the other guys chipped in," Suitcase said, "bought you these."

He took a large bottle of multivitamins from the side pocket of his uniform jacket, handed them to Jesse, and nearly collapsed with laughter.

"Goddamn, Jesse—talk about a cock jockey," Suitcase

struggled to speak through the laughter. "Your ex-wife . . . Marcy Campbell . . . Abby . . . I'm going to start walking . . . my mother . . . to church."

He staggered back against the wall of Jesse's office, now laughing too hard to stand upright. His eyes were wet; his red cheeks were crimson. Jesse smiled and waited for him to get control. Suitcase was only twenty-five. He was a big twenty-five but not a very old one. Molly Crane knocked on the door as she opened it.

"Morris Comden's here, Jesse," she said. "Wants to see you alone."

"Probably looking for sex tips," Suitcase gasped.

"Take Suit out, and send Morris in," Jesse said.

"You give him the vitamins?" Molly said to Suitcase.

Suitcase nodded, and Molly giggled and left the door open as she and Suitcase went out. In a moment Morris Comden came in, glancing back over his shoulder at the two cops who'd just left.

"Must be a hell of a joke, Jess," Comden said.

"Doesn't take a hell of a joke to get those two hysterical," Jesse said. "What's up, Morris?"

Comden looked around the office and glanced back at the half-open door.

"Mind if I close the door, Jess?"

"No."

Comden got up and closed the door and came back and sat down. He hated how Jesse always just answered your question and nothing more.

"We got us a problem, Jess."

Jesse waited.

"You know I've always been in your corner," Comden said.

Jesse waited.

"You remember how I stood with you during the trouble last year," Comden said.

"No, Morris, I don't."

Comden didn't know what to say to that, so he went on as if Jesse hadn't spoken.

"But this is a tough one," Comden said. His voice was

a little hoarse, as if he needed to clear his throat. "Kay Hopkins."

Jesse leaned back in his chair with his elbows resting on the arms of the chair and his fingers laced across his flat stomach.

"You know she's always backed me politically," Comden said.

Jesse nodded.

"And her husband is financially well connected."

"Uh-huh."

Bastard doesn't help you, Morris thought. *He never helps you. He just sits there.*

"Charlie makes a difference in a town like this," Comden said. "And I've been very privileged to call Charlie my friend."

"And supporter," Jesse said.

"Charlie has supported me, and Kay has worked very hard for me."

The office was quiet. Occasionally there was the sound of traffic going by on Summer Street. And the sound of a door shutting somewhere down the hall.

"And, ah, now, damn it, Jess they're asking for my support."

"And?"

"And I think they have a right to it."

Again the room was silent. Jesse was perfectly still in his chair. Comden was unable to say anything else.

Finally Jesse said, "Well if that's all you got to say, Morris, nice talking to you."

"Jess . . . I . . . they, ah, want you to resign."

"I'm sure they do," Jesse said.

"They're adamant."

"I'm sure they are."

"Jesus, Jess . . . Will you resign?"

"No."

"They are prepared to go all the way with it."

"I'm sure they are."

"I . . . I can't promise where I'll come down on this issue, Jess."

"I know where you'll come down, Morris," Jesse said gently. "Without Kay's support and Charlie's money, you can't get elected, and being a selectman in Paradise is the only thing you ever achieved. Otherwise you're just a badly dressed inconsequential dork."

"Jess, you got no business talking to me that way."

"And you'll be trying to get me fired, so Kay Hopkins will be grateful and Charlie Hopkins will help you keep your job and you won't have to go on welfare."

"Jess, damn it, don't you see I'm trying to talk some sense here? You resign. I'll see that you get an excellent recommendation, anywhere you apply."

"There's a couple things, Morris. It will be hard to fire me. Talk with Nick Petrocelli about that. And two, I'm like you. I'm only good at one thing, and this is it. If I'm not doing this, what the hell am I? A guy with a drinking problem that can't get his marriage straightened out."

"I thought you were divorced," Comden said.

"So I'm not going to resign," Jesse said. "Just like you, I'm going to hang on as hard as I can to the only thing that seems to work in my life."

"Well, you don't leave me much choice, Jess."

"I don't have any to leave you, Morris."

"I wish it wasn't this way, Jess."

"Sure."

Comden had risen and was standing uneasily. He had every intention of being tough as nails. But he felt as if Jesse's stare was pushing him backward.

"I hope we're not enemies, Jess."

"The hell we're not," Jesse said.

"We're both just trying to do our job," Comden said.

"Think about it anyway you want, Morris. We're enemies, and I don't want you in my office anymore."

Comden opened his mouth, couldn't think of anything to say, stood there open-mouthed for an indecisive moment, and then turned and went out. Jesse sat staring after him.

"And if you keep calling me Jess," he said out loud in

the empty office, "I'll cut off whatever small balls you have."

Comden didn't hear him, but Jesse liked saying it anyway. It made him smile to himself in the quiet office.

chapter 38

He had them together in Faye's living room for the last meeting.

"You got the bridge rigged?" Macklin said to Fran.

"Yep, JD and I been under there all week."

"How long will it take you to blow?"

"From the time you say go? A minute."

"Yacht club landing?"

"Yep. Pretended I was working on a boat."

"How about the phone lines?" Macklin said.

"Same thing," JD said. "I hit the cut-off switch, and they're dead."

"Which kills the alarms."

"Yes. But it won't kill cell phones," JD said. "Or car phones. You can't cut the island off completely. Somebody's going to make a call."

"It's about odds, JD," Macklin said. "It'll probably be a while before anyone gets to a cell phone. We try to buy as much time as we can before they find out. When they do find out, if we're not done then, Fran dumps the bridge.

Then it'll be another while until they can get boats organized. And it's a lot easier to keep the cops pinned down if they're coming in a boat. Sooner or later they'll get there. But we only need about twenty-four hours. And if we have to, we buy time with hostages. Everything we're doing is temporary. We delay them for a day. We buy ourselves twenty-four hours, and we can clean the island out and be gone. I like our odds."

At the periphery of the group, which was where he always was, Faye thought, Crow smiled slightly, as if he knew a joke no one else knew.

"I don't like our odds," JD said.

"Well, of course," Macklin said. "Nobody likes odds, for crissake. Everybody likes a sure thing. But there isn't any sure thing. All there is are good chances and bad ones. This is a good chance. A good chance here to be rich for the rest of our lives. Is that worth taking a run at?"

"I got four kids," Fran said.

"And you got a chance to make them rich," Macklin said. "We got a great plan, we got the best guys for the job, and it's time to do it."

No one said anything. Crow was still smiling slightly.

"Can't have anybody pulling out now," Macklin said.

"Nobody's pulling out," Fran said.

" 'Course not," Macklin said. "Just the precombat jitters before we hit the beach."

Faye realized suddenly that Crow was looking at her. She met his look, and she realized that he knew what she knew. She knew that Jimmy was never the planner he thought he was, that now he was riding the crest of a manic wave that would sweep him right into the operation. She had tried over the months to rein him in and keep him grounded, but she knew finally she couldn't. He loved the action too much. He loved to be the leader. He loved to think of himself as a kind of master strategist, coolly going into battle with exactly the right troops, with every detail meticulously covered, with the enemy outwitted. But she knew better. Jimmy managed to get the feeling without actually doing it. Like masturbation. And she realized for the first time that Crow knew the same thing she did. That Jimmy was maybe more George Custer than U. S. Grant. Mostly he got by on craziness and courage. The sandwich platter was empty, and Faye picked it up and took it to the kitchen. Crow drifted out behind her and got some ice from the freezer and added it to his glass. He leaned on the counter and sipped his drink.

"Can you pull this off?" Faye said.

Crow shrugged. "Jimmy thinks so," he said.

"Jimmy's enthusiastic," Faye said.

Crow smiled.

"Maybe it's not as sure a thing," Faye said.

"Maybe."

"You scared that it'll go bad?"

"I'm not scared," Crow said.

"But you think it might go bad."

"Might."

"So why are you in it?"

"Why not?" Crow said.

Faye looked at him for a while and knew that there was too big a gulf for her to bridge. All she could do was ask.

"If it goes bad, will you look out for him as much as you can?"

Crow smiled at her.

"Sure," he said.

Faye finished arranging more sandwiches on the platter. Crow swirled the ice slowly in his glass.

"You'd be better off with somebody else, Faye."

"I love him," she said.

"Appears so," Crow said.

They continued to stand, with their private knowledge holding them.

"You're going to go through with it," Faye said.

"Yes."

"Why?"

"Lot of money," Crow said.

"Just that?"

"And I said I would."

"And if it goes bad?"

Crow shrugged and smiled down at her.

"Might be a good day for dying," he said and took a sandwich off the platter.

chapter 39

The condominiums in this part of the Navy Yard were elevated, with parking below. Jesse parked in a space with someone's name and condo number on it, under the building next to the one where Harry Smith's Mercedes was parked. The name on Smith's parking slot was Prentice, and the number was 134. Jesse was driving his own car and wearing jeans and a baseball hat. From where he sat, slouched in the front seat, he could see the front door of condo number 134. He didn't know why he was there exactly. There was just something wrong with Harry Smith. He said he was from Concord, but his car was registered in Charlestown. A lot of people moved without changing their car registration. And the fact that he was parked in a spot that had another name on it was hardly criminal. Maybe his wife kept her maiden name. Maybe the condo was his wife's, and he'd moved in with her when they got married. Which might have been recently. Still it was better to sit here and see what was up with

Harry Smith than sit around the station house taking calls from Abby.

Abby had been ferocious in bed, as if by the force of her desire, she could make him love her. He shouldn't have slept with her. He knew that. It sent her a mixed message. Wiser to have driven her home. But not human. Jesse liked sex, and he accepted as fact that it would sometimes lead him to do things that were unwise. On his deathbed, he was pretty sure, he would not be regretting the women he'd made love with. Abby had cried this morning, full of regret, embarrassed that she'd gotten drunk, frightened of her remembered intensity. Jesse had been steadfast. He had never lied to her, and she knew it. Jesse patted her shoulder and wondered if he'd sleep with her again.

A tall, bony guy with red hair pulled back in a ponytail stepped out onto the small wooden entry porch of condo 134 and lit a cigarette. Thank you for not smoking.

Whether he would sleep with Abby again was not pressing. He was after all also sleeping with Marcy and at least once with Jenn. Probably he would sleep with Jenn again. One was never sure about anything with Jenn, except that the prospect of sex with her made all other sex merely a speculative abstraction. He smiled to himself. It was easier to think calmly about sex when it was abundant.

The door to condo 134 opened, and Mrs. Smith came out and handed the red-haired guy a drink. Mrs. Smith was good-looking. Jesse smiled at himself again. The appeal of strange stuff. It would be fun to party with friends in the late afternoon like that and stand on the porch and have a drink and look at the harbor. The red-haired guy took a last drag on his cigarette, flipped it into the ocean, and followed Mrs. Smith inside. The door closed. Jesse looked at his watch. It was getting on toward cocktail time for him. He could wait. And when he got home, he could have a couple. Having a couple of drinks at night gave him something to look forward to all day. And no harm to it, as long as he controlled it. He seemed to be controlling it, mostly. He was pretty sure he wasn't an alcoholic, or at least not an alcoholic anymore. If he could get really in comfortable control, he'd be halfway home. Then all he'd have to do was get in control of Jenn . . . or himself. Maybe, if he got really in control of himself, he wouldn't have to control Jenn. He could control his reaction to her. And if he could do that, he thought maybe he wouldn't have to be so much of a cop so much of the time.

The door opened again, and four men came out of condo 134. One of them was the red-haired guy; another one might have been an American Indian. There was something about the Indian. They got in a maroon Chevrolet van and drove away. The van had Arizona plates. Jesse took down the number. Just because he was there and he could. Just gathering information. *That's like a cop's job description,* Jesse thought, *just gathering information.* Is it important? I don't know. Can you use it? Beats me. Why do it? Why not.

Jesse stayed where he was until after 7:00. Neither of the Smiths came out. Jesse needed a drink. And he had a date. He started up and drove down the wharf, and past the navy yard where the marine sentries still stood guard. At City Square, where the density of the old city had been leveled as part of a project begun before Jesse had come east, he went over the Charlestown Bridge and turned right onto Causeway Street, where they were tearing down the Boston Garden, past the single tenement left from the west end reclamation that had been completed long before Jesse came east. He saw nothing that made him optimistic about future reclamations. He went behind the new Fleet Center and past the old registry building and the old Suffolk County Jail now defunct, under the up ramp to the central artery, which was heading for extinction, and onto Storrow Drive. The Charles River was on his right. He hadn't been east that long but he had learned to like the river, the city, which had been old when Los Angeles was founded. He turned off Storrow at the Arlington Street exit. He found a parking space on Jenn's street and walked toward Jenn's apartment in the pleasant darkness, just like a regular suitor.

chapter 40

Marcy Campbell had just unlocked the office when Harry Smith came in with an interesting-looking man who might have been an American Indian. He was carrying a long gym bag. Marcy was not particularly pleased to see Harry Smith. She was beginning to think he was a deadbeat. A guy who looked and never bought, maybe even, a guy who looked, never bought, and merely wished to core the real estate lady. Oh well.

"Good morning, Harry," Marcy said.

"Hi, Marcy."

He turned the OPEN/CLOSED sign in the front window to CLOSED, closed the venetian blinds, took a 9-mm pistol from under his coat, and pointed it at her.

"Get up please, Marcy, and lie facedown on the couch."

"Harry, what the hell are you doing?" she said.

"Just do what I tell you, and quickly."

The interesting Indian-looking man put a long gym bag down beside the couch. Then he straightened and looked at her without any expression.

"Why do you want me to lie on the couch?" Marcy felt the bottom of her stomach begin to sag.

"You weren't so slow to flop last time I saw you, Marce," Harry said. "Crow."

The Indian stepped over to the desk, took Marcy's arm, jerked her out of the chair, and spun her onto the couch facedown. He held her there with one hand between her shoulder blades while he took some rope from the gym bag. Quickly he tied her hands behind her back. She could feel her skirt gathered halfway up her thighs. When he finished tying her hands he smoothed the skirt down to where it belonged and then tied her ankles together.

"Harry, why are you doing this?" Marcy said. She could feel the panic rising in her throat. "What are you going to do to me?"

"Already did it, Marce, already did it," Harry said.

He was looking out the window through the small space between the blind and the casement frame. The Indian took some gray duct tape from the bag, tore off a strip, and taped her mouth shut. He put the rope and the duct tape neatly back in the bag and, without any apparent effort, turned her over onto her back. He slid one of the couch pillows under her head and adjusted her so that she looked comfortable. Then he picked up the gym bag and went to the window where Harry was standing. He took a shotgun out of the gym bag. Harry turned from the window and the Indian replaced him. Harry came and sat on the edge of the couch where Marcy lay.

"You breathe all right?" Harry said.

Marcy nodded.

"Good. You have any trouble, make some noise, and we'll check on you," Harry said. "We're going to be here for a while. Use this as sort of a headquarters. I don't think you'll have to be tied up too long."

He stood and went to the washroom and looked in. There was no window. He turned back to Marcy.

"You got to go to the bathroom, make some noise about that. We'll untie you and let you close the door. You understand?"

Marcy nodded.

"Fine."

Harry turned away and went and sat in the swivel chair behind Marcy's desk. He put the pistol on the desk, looked at his watch, picked up the phone, and dialed.

"It's me," he said into the phone. "We're here, and we're set up."

He listened.

"Okay," he said. "You got this number, right . . . Say it . . . Okay . . . You need to, call me here."

He hung up and looked at the Indian.

"The dance has started," Harry said.

His eyes were bright, Marcy thought, as if he had a fever. Still looking out the window, the Indian nodded without speaking. *Maybe it's not me,* Marcy thought. *Maybe they are going to do something else.*

chapter 41

The maroon Chevrolet van was registered to Wilson Cromartie of Tucson. Suitcase Simpson came in with the information and sat down across from Jesse. He was bulky enough so that the chair was a tight fit, and he had to adjust his gun forward a little to get comfortable.

"Guy lives off Swan Road," Jesse said.

"That mean something?"

"Good neighborhood," Jesse said.

"You know Tucson?"

"Grew up there. My old man was with the Sheriff's Department."

"Cochise County?" Suitcase said.

"Everybody knows Cochise County," Jesse said.

"Least I know one," Suitcase said.

"Cochise is down around Tombstone," Jesse said. "My old man was Pima County."

"You know anybody there still?" Suitcase said.

"Uh-huh."

"Maybe you should call him up and see what he knows about Wilson Cromartie."

"You think?" Jesse said.

"Sure, I mean if something's going on and we don't . . . ah shit, you're kidding me again, aren't you?"

"Only a little," Jesse said. He leaned forward and shouted for Molly to come in from the front desk.

"I want to talk to a Pima County, Arizona, sheriff's deputy named Travis Randall," Jesse said. "He knew my father. He'll remember me."

"I'm on it," Molly said.

When she left, Suitcase looked after her.

"I believe you were eying Molly's ass," Jesse said.

Suitcase reddened. "So?"

"She's married and has two kids, Suit."

"Doesn't make her ass ugly," Suitcase said.

"Good point."

In ten minutes, Molly stuck her head into Jesse's office.

"Lieutenant Travis Randall on line one, Jesse."

Jesse picked up.

"Travis?" he said.

"Jesse, how ya doing?"

"You got promoted."

"Had to happen sooner or later," Randall said. "Hell you got to be chief."

"Says so right on my desk plate," Jesse said.

"Your old man still around?"

"No."

"Sorry to hear that."

"Thanks, he's been gone a while. I'm looking for anything you might be able to tell me about a guy named Wilson Cromartie. Lives in Tucson."

Jesse gave him the street address.

"Familiar name," Randall said. "Lemme punch him up here."

"You're working a computer, Travis?"

"Goes to show you," Randall said. "You can teach an old dog new tricks."

"Guess so. I'm going to put you on speaker phone."

"Sure."

Jesse punched the speaker phone button and hung up the receiver. Suitcase sat across the desk from him, listening to the airy silence of the speaker phone. Being a policeman excited him. Working on even the small-town cases he got to work on was thrilling to him, and he watched Jesse who had been a big city cop in Los Angeles as if he were magical. Randall's voice came back.

"Yep, that's him. Crow."

"Short for Cromartie?"

"I suppose," Randall said. "But he spells it C-R-O-W. Claims he's an Apache Indian."

"Is he?"

"Could be. You can see Indian in him."

"Tell me about him," Jesse said.

"He's a bad man," Randall said. "Contract killer."

"Connected with anybody?"

"Freelance. He's good. Gets plenty of work."

"Warrants?"

"Nothing outstanding," Randall said. "Hard to get anyone to say anything about Crow."

"You got a description?"

"Black hair, brown eyes. Six feet, hundred and ninety pounds. Muscular. Indian features. Very neat. You seen him or just the car?"

"I saw him," Jesse said.

"Be very fucking careful of him, Jesse."

"Sure."

"Whether he's got a gun or not," Randall said.

"Okay. You got any idea what he might be doing here?"

" 'Here' is around Boston?"

"Yeah."

"Not that I know about. Lemme look some more."

Again Jesse and Suitcase listened to the sound of silence running along the wires from Arizona.

"Here's something," Randall said. "He was convicted of armed robbery along with a guy named James Macklin. Knocked over a liquor store in Flagstaff. Macklin is listed as being from Dorchester, Mass."

"Part of Boston," Jesse said. "They do time?"

"Three years in Yuma."

"Both get out?"

"Far as I know."

"Anything else on Macklin?"

"Nope."

"Description?"

"Nope."

"Okay, Travis, thank you."

"No problem," Randall said. "I'll keep sniffing around out here. I come across anything else, I'll call you."

"Do that," Jesse said.

"And Jesse, don't you or anyone try to take Crow alone. He don't care if you're a cop or not."

"Would you try to take him alone, Travis?"

"Absolutely not."

"We'll be cool," Jesse said.

"And don't be a stranger, boy. Your father and I was pretty tight. Betty and me be happy to have you visit."

"Thanks, Travis. I'll keep it in mind."

Jesse leaned over and switched off the speaker.

"Suit," Jesse said. "See what you can come up with on James Macklin of Dorchester."

"Whaddya think is going down, Jesse?"

"Maybe they're just having a reunion, Yuma, class of eighty-eight," Jesse said. "Maybe it's got nothing to do with us."

"I'll bet it's the Paradise Bank, Jesse. I'll bet they're going to knock over the bank."

"We're not supposed to bet, Suit. We're supposed to find out. So go find out about James Macklin of Dorchester, Mass."

Suitcase stood up.

"Yessir, chief," he said.

"And you heard what Randall said about Crow. If Randall wouldn't go him alone . . ."

"Randall a tough guy?" Suitcase said.

"You have no idea," Jesse said.

Suitcase nodded and headed to the door, then stopped as if he'd forgotten something.

"Oh, chief ?"

"Yeah?"

"You taking your vitamins?"

"And eating a lot of oysters," Jesse said.

Red-faced with delight at his own joke, Suitcase went out the door.

chapter 42

It was 9:00 A.M. when Freddie Costa pulled the big power boat away from the town landing in Paradise Harbor and began to move slowly among the moored sailboats toward the buoys that marked the channel. He had a full tank of gas, and the engine was tuned. A Winchester rifle lay in its rack above the door. There was no need to hide it. A lot of people on the ocean carried a rifle with them. He sipped coffee from a big plastic mug. The sun was bright, coming in from his right, over the rooftops of Paradise Neck, as he headed north toward the harbor mouth. The wind was off the water, blowing straight toward him, and it raised a short chop that made the bow pound as he drove slowly through it. He didn't mind the chop. He'd been on the ocean most of his life, since his father used to take him out on the scallop draggers from New Bedford. He liked the ocean. He liked it best when he was alone on it, and the sun was out, like today, and fragments of it were ricocheting off the water. Some gulls trailed the boat hopefully for a while, but when there was no food forthcoming, they peeled off and went back to foraging around the restaurant on the wharf.

It would take awhile, with the headwind, to beat out of the harbor and around to the other side of Stiles Island. That was okay. He didn't have to get there soon. It might not be until tomorrow that he would take them out. He'd idle off-shore, maybe drop anchor for a while, and then when the flare went up, he'd pull in and they'd wade out to him. Then he would take them up around Cape Ann and put them ashore north of Port City, where Faye would be waiting with the van. He'd keep going north, maybe to Portsmouth, and lay up for a while until everything calmed down. Then he'd head back south to Mattapoisett with his money and maybe do some sport fishing.

As he stood at the wheel, he could feel the faint comforting vibration of the big engine. The boat was neat. The ropes coiled. Everything polished. To his right, the big homes on the neck had lawns that sloped to the water. In most cases, they were sustained by massive seawalls. Often there were stairs cut into the seawalls, and small boats bobbing below them at wooden floats. To his left the town rose idiosyncratically. A jumble of church spires and eighteenth-century buildings ascending Indian Hill. The big square steeple of the town hall, with the big clock face on all four sides, rose above most of the buildings halfway up the hill. On top of the hill, Costa could see the green mass of the park.

The boat pushed on out of the harbor mouth past Stiles Island, barely tethered to Paradise Neck by the small bridge. *Nice-looking bridge,* Costa thought. Costa liked constructs: engines, bridges, buildings, ships. *Too bad about the bridge,* he thought. The houses on Stiles were even bigger than the houses on Paradise Neck, but there was less variety. From the harbor, as Costa chugged past them, they looked nearly the same, with only an occasional variation in the color of the siding or the shingles. Past Stiles Island point, Costa turned the boat east and ran it straight toward the morning sun along the north shore of Stiles.

He used to bring a dog on board with him, but his wife had gotten the dog when she divorced him, along with almost everything but the boat. It was all right. He could get another dog. Get a purebred this time, a big dog, maybe one of those Dalmatians. He liked Dalmatians. He was planning to have one by now, but he couldn't bring a new dog on board for a deal like this. He'd get it when he went home. Get a male. Be a good watchdog for the boat. Off the right side of the boat, he saw the cove, down past the seaside restaurant with its big picture windows, bright and blank with reflected sunlight. He throttled back to idle and let the boat drift awhile with the wind and the chop. There was no sign of activity. Nothing was happening on the island. He looked at his watch. 10:10 A.M. Macklin was scheduled to have set up by now on the island, and Macklin was big for schedules. Costa smiled a little. *Or he says he is,* Costa thought.

chapter 43

Jesse drove up to talk with Harry Smith. He brought
Suitcase Simpson with him and Anthony DeAngelo. Both
of them wore vests and carried shotguns. If Travis Randall
was afraid of the Indian, Jesse would be too.

"Stand by in the car," Jesse said. "If I get scared, I'll
holler."

Walking up the stairs to the front door of condo 134, he
could feel the muscles tighten across the back of his shoulders. He'd seen some scary gangbangers in South Central
L.A., but there was something about the way Randall had
talked about the Indian.

Mrs. Smith answered the door. Jesse was not in uniform, and she drew a blank at first. He showed her his
shield.

"Jesse Stone," he said. "Paradise Police."

Faye felt a stab of fear run the length of her gut.

"Oh, yes," she said. "Chief Stone. What brings you
here?"

"Well I was hoping to talk with Mr. Smith. Is he home?"

What did he want? Why was he here? The thing on Stiles Island had already started. How could it be a coincidence? She had to make him talk. She had to know.

"No, I'm sorry. He's not, may I help you with something?"

Faye noticed that there were at least two more cops below in the cruiser.

"I don't know," Jesse said. "May I come in?"

"Of course."

She stepped away from the door, and Jesse went into the apartment. The wall opposite was all glass and looked straight out onto Boston Harbor, with the Boston skyline across the water. The doorway to the bedroom was ajar, and Jesse noticed that the ceiling was mirrored. *Atta girl, Mrs. Smith.* She was a good-looking woman. Nice body, looked strong.

"Coffee?" she said. "Or something stronger? I suppose I shouldn't say that, should I? You being a policeman on duty and such."

She did the fluttery housewife thing pretty well, Jesse thought, but if you paid attention there were a lot of little details that suggested strength, not flutter.

"Nothing, thank you, Mrs. Smith. May I sit?"

"Of course. Please call me Rocky."

"Short for?"

"Roxanne," she said.

Jesse nodded. Faye marveled at how she'd pulled "Roxanne" out of the air. What the hell would "Rocky" be short for?

"Do you know anyone named Wilson Cromartie?" Jesse said.

"Wilson Cromartie, no. I can't say I do," she said.

It was an easy lie for Faye because when he said the name, it didn't mean anything. Only as she was saying it over, did she realize that it was Crow.

"Maybe you don't know him by that name," Jesse said.

"He's an American Indian. Says he's Apache, calls himself Crow."

"I'm sorry, Chief Stone. I really don't know anyone like that."

Jesse nodded again. He was pleasant and easy speaking. But Jimmy had said he was more than he seemed.

"How about anyone named James Macklin?" Jesse said.

Jesus Christ. Faye felt the thrill of fear jag through her intestines. *How much does he know?*

"I don't think so," she said.

"You're not sure?"

"Yes, I'm sure. It's just that you meet so many people . . ."

"A maroon Chevy van registered to Wilson Cromartie was parked underneath this condo Sunday night, and three men, one of whom appeared to be an American Indian, came out of this condo and got into the van and drove away."

He knows something's up, Faye thought. *But he doesn't know what. If he knew what, he wouldn't waste time talking to me like this.*

"They were here to see Harry," she said. "I don't think he knew them very well."

"What were they here to see Harry about?"

"I don't know. They had some sort of business proposal. I believe Harry wasn't interested."

"What's Harry's business?" Jesse said.

Mrs. Smith smiled. "He always says he's like a strapless gown—no visible means of support," she said. "I guess you'd say he was an entrepreneur. Real estate. Banking. Stocks and bonds. Buys a business, builds it up, sells it at a profit. I frankly don't pay a bunch of attention to my husband's businesses."

"Wilson Cromartie is a career criminal," Jesse said.

"He is? My God. I didn't spend any time with them, but he seemed perfectly nice when I let them in."

"I thought you should know," Jesse said.

"I'll tell Harry. Maybe he knows. Maybe that's why he wouldn't do business with them."

Jesse sat quietly looking at her. Everything she said was plausible. And Jesse didn't believe any of it. Something was going on. But he had no basis to arrest her or search her home or do anything else but what he'd done. He took a card from his shirt pocket and handed it to Mrs. Smith.

"Please ask your husband to give me a call when he comes in," Jesse said.

She put the card down, face up, on the glass-topped coffee table.

"Of course," she said.

Jesse stood. She stood with him and walked with him to the door.

Driving out of the Navy Yard, Suitcase glanced at Jesse.

"Just the woman in there?"

Jesse nodded.

"So you didn't need us?"

"Nope, I was able to hold her at bay."

They were quiet as they drove toward City Square. Jesse sat beside Suitcase. Anthony DeAngelo sat in back.

"You happen to fuck her, Jesse?" Anthony said.

"Not this time," Jesse said.

"Good to know there's someone," Anthony said.

He and Suitcase chortled lengthily as the cruiser turned onto the ramp and headed north over the Tobin Bridge.

Jesse said, "You guys have little interest in making sergeant, I assume."

This made both of them chortle harder, as the cruiser headed back to Paradise.

chapter 44

Nothing had happened to her, and maybe nothing would. Harry and the Indian had paid no more attention to her as she lay on the couch. Two other men came in. Would they do something to her? The taller of the new men had a red ponytail; the other one was smaller and had his black hair slicked into a ducktail. *My God, a ducktail!* Both men looked at her curiously.

"Dessert?" JD said to Macklin.

Marcy felt the terror again, rippling through her like an electric serpent.

"Leave her alone," Macklin said.

"Shame to waste her," JD said.

"You touch her, and you'll have to explain it to Crow after we're finished," Macklin said.

JD looked at Crow. Crow glanced at him for a moment. JD made a motion that might have been a shrug or a shiver.

"She's safe with me," JD said.

"She better be," Macklin said. "I'm going to ask her when we come back."

Marcy felt the serpent again. They had come in here and pointed a gun at her and tied her up and gagged her, but she had already begun to see them as protectors. She didn't want them to leave her with these other men. She made a noise.

"You breathing okay?" Macklin said.

She nodded.

"Want to go to the bathroom?"

Marcy shook her head.

"You're scared of these guys," Macklin said. "No need. They won't touch you, will they Crow?"

"They won't," Crow said.

Marcy could hear in his voice what the two men heard, and she realized they wouldn't dare cross him. She felt grateful to the Indian.

"Sit tight," Macklin said to Fran and JD. "Don't answer the phone unless it's me. Monitor the calls on the answering machine. We'll be back in half an hour."

Mr. Smith and the Indian went out the door and Marcy was alone with the two strange men. They both looked at her silently for a moment and then ignored her.

The Stiles Island Patrol was part of a security company called Citadel Security, which was run by a former Marine captain named Kurt Billups. Billups dressed his men like drill instructors complete with campaign hats tilted sharply down over their noses. There were no fat, aging rent-a-cops on the Stiles Island Patrol. All his men were trim and neat. Their pistol belts were polished. Their shoes gleamed. The khaki shirts had military creases in them. The red and white Ford sedans they drove were always clean. Like most of the patrol, Michael Deering and Dan Moncrief were Marine Corps veterans. Deering had been to the Gulf. Moncrief had spent his full enlistment in San Diego. Deering was driving, and both were drinking the first coffee of the day as they came over the hill on Sea Street with the morning sun warming the car.

They were on the seaward side of Stiles Island, at the

point farthest from the bridge. There was a long section of Sea Street reserved as green space by the resort planners. There were no houses on that section, and the trees came down to either side of the road. Kids used it sometimes to drink beer and smoke pot. And people with dogs brought them here to let them run despite the Island leash law. This morning there was a maroon Chevy van skidded off the road, and a man lying in the street beside it. As Deering and Moncrief drove toward the scene, a man struggled out of the van and crouched beside the prone figure. Deering pulled over on the opposite side of the street, and he and Moncrief got out and walked across.

"What happened?" Deering said.

The man on the ground rolled over onto his back and shot Deering through the forehead. Moncrief didn't even get his hand onto his gun before the man on the ground shot him through the forehead too.

"Nice," Macklin said.

Crow got up, let the hammer down on his gun, dropped the magazine from the handle, methodically replaced the two rounds, slapped the magazine back up into the handle, and holstered the weapon. Then he and Macklin pulled the two dead men by their ankles into the woods. Macklin stripped the uniform shirt from Deering. Crow began to cover them with leaves and branches. Macklin drove the patrol car into the woods on the other side of the street and piled boughs they had already cut to conceal it.

They got into the van together, Macklin driving, and pulled away. The killings and concealment had taken three minutes and eight seconds.

"Gatekeeper?" Crow said.

"Yep."

"Who you going to put in there?"

"On the bridge? Fran. He says he can blow the bridge from there."

"Perfect."

chapter 45

Jesse was in the donut shop with Suitcase Simpson. Suitcase had two Boston cream donuts on a paper plate in front of him.

"Suit, those things will kill you," Jesse said.

"Then I'll go happy," Suitcase said and put half of the first donut into his mouth. As he chewed, he fished in his shirt pocket and got out his notebook. Suitcase put the notebook on the counter and leafed through it with his left hand while he held the donut in his right, leaning over the counter so that it wouldn't leak onto his notebook.

When he got enough of the donut chewed and swallowed, Suitcase said, "I got some stuff on this guy Macklin."

Jesse sipped his coffee. It was 10:00 in the morning. The donut shop was almost empty after the early commuter rush, and the counter people were bustling around cleaning up napkins and newspapers and throwing away stray paper cups. A guy in a white apron and tee shirt brought out a big basket of new donuts, and the smell of them mixed happily with the scent of coffee.

"Macklin's a career criminal," Suit said. "Mostly armed robbery. Got out of MCI Concord about six months ago. Done time in Arizona and Florida and Michigan. Got a girlfriend named Faye Valentine been with him as far back as we go."

"Description?"

"Better," Suitcase said and produced a mug shot.

"Harry Smith," Jesse said.

Suitcase nodded. He was proud of any detective work he did, even if it were simply back-checking. Jesse handed the picture back to Suitcase.

"Nice work, Suit," he said.

Suitcase's naturally high color deepened. "There's more," he said. "There's a notation that anybody got information on Macklin should contact a homicide detective at Boston Police Headquarters."

"Which you did," Jesse said.

"Yeah, I went to see him."

Jesse knew that Suitcase could have called, but the chance to go into the big city police station and talk with the big city homicide cop, man to man, was more than the kid could resist. It made Jesse want to smile. But he didn't. And it wasn't a bad thing for a young cop to be excited by the job. Suitcase took a moment to finish his first donut. He wiped some cream filling off the corner of his mouth.

"Sergeant named Belson," Suitcase said. "Been trying to catch Macklin for ten, fifteen years, he said."

"Homicide cop?"

"Yeah. Says he knows Macklin murdered some people but he can't prove it, and he has taken, like, a personal interest."

"Macklin's his hobby," Jesse said.

Suitcase looked at Jesse with nearly blatant admiration. "Yeah, that's just the expression Belson used. Hobby. Macklin is his personal hobby, he said."

Jesse nodded. He knew that Suit would file that phrase and eventually somewhere in his career would use it, and, because he was going to be a good cop, would in fact make somebody his personal hobby some day.

"He tell you about it?"

"Yeah. He says Macklin's a stone killer. Says there was a hostage situation in a liquor store heist couple years back in Brighton, before Macklin went to Concord. Robber held the clerk and two customers hostage when a silent alarm tripped and the cops showed up and caught him in the act. Store was in a mall, and they sealed off the front and the back. But he apparently found a way out by going through the cellar and up the stairs into one of those discount department stores next door. Nobody ever got a good look at the robber, except the hostages. When our side got in, the hostages were shot dead and the perp was gone."

"Belson thinks it was Macklin."

"Says he knows it was. Says a snitch he trusts told him off the record. But he could never come up with anything other than the snitch's word, and the snitch wouldn't testify."

"Scared of Macklin?"

"Terrified, Belson says. And even if he wasn't, it wouldn't be enough. It's hearsay."

"Why's he so sure it's Macklin?"

"He was in the area. They've established that. He's living good with no visible means. Weapon was a nine-millimeter handgun. Not a rarity, but Macklin's gun of choice. And, Belson says, it's Macklin's style. He doesn't mind killing people. Back as far as Belson can trace him, he's solved his problems by shooting them. Doesn't seem to bother him at all."

"Belson know anything about Wilson Cromartie?"

"No."

"Anything about Faye what's-her-last-name?"

Suitcase checked his notebook. "Valentine," he said. "Just that he knows that she's been with him a long time."

"Odd a guy like that is faithful," Jesse said.

"Maybe he ain't," Suitcase said. "Maybe she is."

Suitcase was getting older every day, Jesse thought.

"Belson got any thoughts on what Macklin might be doing in Paradise?"

"Nothing legal. Belson's been chasing him for years, says he knows him better than he knows his wife. Says he's a crook because he's good at it and he likes the hours, but also because he's a thrill junkie."

Jesse nodded.

"Sorta like you said about him flirting with you," Suitcase said.

"Sort of," Jesse said.

"Belson says anything he'd be happy to help anyway he can."

Jesse nodded.

"And he said another thing," Suitcase looked a little uneasy and braced himself with a mouthful of Boston cream donut. "He said if we got a chance to arrest Macklin and he were, ah, killed resisting, that wouldn't be a bad thing. He said it would be a very efficient thing."

Suitcase took another bite of donut.

"He asked me to tell you that too," Suitcase said.

"Sounds like Macklin has been his hobby too long," Jesse said.

"I asked him if it was personal," Suitcase said. "And he looked kind of mad when I asked him, but all he said was that one of the hostages Macklin killed was twenty-two years old and pregnant."

Jesse nodded and finished his coffee.

"Well," Jesse said, "we'll keep it in mind."

chapter 46

When he got back to the station, Molly was waiting for him.

"Talk, Jesse, alone?"

"Sure."

They went into his office and closed the door. Molly was carrying a small notebook.

"You tell your ex-wife about Mrs. Hopkins trying to get you fired?" Molly said.

"Christ, what did she do?" Jesse said.

Molly smiled without any pleasure. "She assaulted Mrs. Hopkins."

Jesse leaned back in his chair and stared at Molly without speaking. He was thrilled that Jenn cared enough about him to do that. He was annoyed that he would have to deal with it. He was depressed that Jenn was still so far out of control that she would assault someone. He was amused at the image of her in full assault.

"Where is she now?" Jesse said.

"Down the hall," Molly said. "Cell number one."

Jesse nodded slowly. Molly couldn't tell what he was thinking.

"Tell me about it," he said.

"Well," Molly said. "Kay Hopkins was at the women's Republican breakfast at the Village Room. She was supposed to give a report on her committee's findings about citizen participation in town government. It was in *The Shopper's News,* maybe that's where Jenn saw it. Anyway, she shows up. And when Kay Hopkins gets up to give her report, Jenn gets up and says," Molly looked down at her notes, " 'Before you give your report, maybe you ought to explain to these ladies why you are interfering with the police department in the performance of its lawful duties.' "

Jesse leaned back in his chair and closed his eyes.

" 'Lawful duties,' " he said softly.

Molly was still reading from her notes.

"And Kay Hopkins says, 'The chair has not recognized you. Please sit down and be quiet.' "

"Uh-oh!" Jesse said softly.

"You got that right," Molly said. "Jenn calls her a bitch. Mrs. Hopkins says something like 'How dare you talk to me that way?' And Jenn marches up and whacks her across the face and everybody starts screaming and pushing and shoving and people are trying to help Mrs. Hopkins and somebody calls us. Peter Perkins was there because he was in the nearest cruiser, and when he got there he saw it was a woman and asked me to come."

"And?"

Molly tried to control a smile. "And it wasn't a pretty sight. Jenn had torn most of Mrs. Hopkins' blouse off and given her a bloody nose. Mrs. Hopkins has got blood all over her skirt and her bra, which looked, may I add, as if it had been laundered a couple times too often. Jenn's got blood all over her blouse. As far as I know she's not hurt. It's Hopkins' blood, I'm pretty sure. There were two or three women trying to hold onto Jenn, who was kicking people and, as I arrived, was actually head-butting Gertrude Richardson, who's the chairwoman or whatever they call her. Peter Perkins wasn't exactly sure what he was supposed to do and looked so grateful when I showed up. I thought he was going to kiss me."

"You get her calmed down?"

"No, not really. Peter and I had to pretty well wrestle her down, and I had to cuff her before we could get her under control. Thing is neither Peter nor I recognized her at first. I seen her on TV a couple times after Suitcase told me she was your ex-wife and she was a weather girl."

"Curiosity," Jesse said.

"Absolutely," Molly said. "But, you know, her hair was mussed and her shirttail was hanging out and one of her high heels was broken off and she didn't look the same. But man can she swear. She called Mrs. Hopkins stuff I haven't even heard around the station. And I've heard a lot around the station."

"Jenn was always a good swearer," Jesse said. "She tell you she was my wife—ex-wife?"

"Yes. When we got her in the cruiser and were bringing her back. The restaurant is going to bring some sort of charge once their attorney tells them what it is. I think she broke a table and certainly some crockery. I can talk to the owner. I know her. I think she'll back off when she finds out the whole story."

"Mrs. Hopkins planning to press charges?" Jesse said.

"Oh, I imagine," Molly said. "And she probably won't back off."

Jesse nodded as much to himself as to Molly.

"Be a surprise if she did," he said. "How is Jenn now?"

"Scared I think," Molly said. "But still mad as hell."

"She's sort of a television celebrity," Jesse said. "The press showed up yet?"

"Not yet."

"She want to see me?" Jesse said.

"Yes."

Jesse took in a long breath.

"Okay, I'll go down and talk to her. Alone."

"Of course," Molly said.

She left the office. Jesse sat for a moment. Then he took

a bottle of Irish whisky from his desk, poured some into a paper cup, looked at it for a moment, and then drank it. He crumpled up the paper cup and threw it into the waste basket. He put the bottle back in the desk drawer. Then he stood and walked down the corridor toward the holding cells.

chapter **47**

Macklin left the real estate office at 9:35 P.M. and walked toward the guard shack at the bridge fifty yards away. Crow walked with him. J. T. McGonigle, who had been there the first time Macklin came to Stiles Island, was on duty again. He was not cut from Captain Billups' pattern. He was what the captain considered "a civilian employee." While he had on the tan regulation uniform shirt, he wore no hat, and he carried no weapon. If there was trouble, he called the patrol.

Macklin spoke to him as he reached the shack.

"How you doing, Mac?"

McGonigle put his clipboard down. There were no cars coming in either direction.

"Good, Mr. Smith, whaddya need?"

"Just wanted to say good-bye," Macklin said and shot McGonigle in the forehead.

He stepped away as McGonigle started to fall. Crow stepped in and caught McGonigle on his shoulder and picked him up. Fran, carrying a briefcase and a folding sign, came from the real estate office as soon as he heard the shot. As Crow carried J. T. McGonigle away, Fran, wearing the tan shirt of the dead Michael Deering, placed the sign in the roadway by the gate and slipped into the guard shack.

Fran took a small remote control mechanism that looked like a garage door opener from the briefcase and put it on the counter beside the clipboard. He brought out a cellular phone and put it beside the remote. He took a big stainless steel Ruger .357 Magnum revolver with a walnut handle from the briefcase and laid it beside the phone. Finally, he placed a pair of binoculars beside the Ruger.

Crow reached the real estate office and bent forward and allowed McGonigle's dead body to slide to the ground, where it was concealed by two decorative cedar shrubs behind the building. Then he went back into the real estate office and waited for Macklin.

JD was sitting at the desk, toying with two cellular phones on the desk in front of him, turning them idly, in slow circles. On the couch Marcy was trying not to look at anything. Nice-looking woman, Crow thought. Macklin came back into the real estate office.

"Okay," Macklin said. "We got the bridge secured. JD, you ready to kibosh the phones?"

"Five minutes," JD said, "from whenever you say."

"After you do it," Crow said, "what do I hear, I try to use the phone?"

"Busy signal," JD said, "either way. Calling in, calling out. People call, get a busy signal, hang up. Be a while before anyone catches on that something's wrong.

"Every minute we can buy, helps us," Macklin said.

He looked at his watch.

"I got seven minutes before ten. Crow and I are going to start rounding people up at ten-fifteen. I want the phone lines fucked by then."

"Easy," JD said.

"Once you fuck the phone lines, you can cut Marcy loose. But keep her here. She wants her purse, give it to her. I've already checked it. She can go in the lav and lock the door, she wants. There's no window."

"Be easier to leave her like she is," JD said. "Then I don't have to watch her."

"We want you to do it our way," Macklin said. "Don't we, Crow?"

"We do," Crow said and held JD's look until JD looked away.

JD shrugged as if Crow didn't scare him, which Crow did. And both of them knew it.

"Sure thing," JD said.

Macklin picked up one of the cell phones and followed Crow out the door.

chapter 48

"We've got to stop meeting this way," Jenn said when Jesse came in.

She was sitting on the cot, with her feet tucked up under her. Jesse left the cell door open and leaned against the wall opposite her. The cell was so small there was barely any space between them.

"I don't know what to say."

"I couldn't stand it," Jenn said. "It's not fair—that bitch trying to take you down. You're so good, Jesse."

"Thank you, Jenn."

"It's the truth. They're lucky to have you. She should be grateful. They all should be grateful."

"Actually Jenn, I'm a little grateful to be here. I almost flushed myself in L.A."

"I know. I helped with that."

"Maybe not as much as you think."

"Have I fucked you up again?" Jenn said.

Jesse smiled. "God, Jenn, I don't know. I mean, thank

you for caring and for standing up for me. But now you're in my jail, and I have no idea what to do with you."

"You could just let me go."

"Yeah."

"But if you did, then Mrs. Bitch Face could accuse you of favoritism."

"Yeah."

"What would happen if I weren't me?" Jenn asked.

"You'd call your lawyer, and your lawyer would arrange your release."

"I don't have a lawyer."

"I could ask Abby Taylor," Jesse said.

"Didn't you fuck her?"

"Uh-huh."

Jesse decided not to mention how recently. Jenn was shaking her head.

"No. I can't have her."

"Station got a lawyer?" Jesse asked.

"Yes. I suppose they'll have him out here as soon as they get wind of it. I may have made myself some trouble at the station."

Jesse smiled.

"Might be your big break," Jesse said. "Jenn Stone, the fighting weather girl?"

"I better tell the station," Jenn said. "Can I use your phone to call the news director?"

"Sure. You're free to go, Jenn."

"Won't you get in trouble, just letting me go like that?"

"If I do, I'll deal with it when it comes. I'm not going to lock you up."

Jenn sat for a moment without moving, and Jesse realized she was crying.

"Oh, shit," Jesse said.

"Here we are together, talking in a jail cell, Jesse," Jenn said. "It's just so . . ."

"Not the way we first planned it," Jesse said.

"God, I've made such a goddamned mess of everything."

"It's not over," Jesse said, "until it's over."

"What the hell does that mean?"

"It means we're working on it, Jenn. When we're through working on it, we'll find out if it's a mess or not."

"I don't ever want to stop working on it," Jenn said. "I don't want to lose you."

"You won't lose me," Jesse said.

"But I don't know. I don't know if I can ever be what you want me to be."

"I don't have any big rules about what you should be, Jenn. Mostly I'm opposed to sharing you."

"I don't know," Jenn said. "I just don't know."

"You will," Jesse said.

"I only know I can't imagine a world without you in it."

"I'm not going anywhere," Jesse said. "I'm going to wait it out."

"God, I hope it's not a long wait," Jenn said.

"You seeing a shrink these days?"

"Dr. St. Claire gave me the name of two people — one in Chestnut Hill, one in Cambridge. I haven't called them. It's hard to go to a new shrink."

"I imagine it would be," Jesse said.

"You think I should go back into therapy?"

"Anything that will help you decide what you want to do, and then be able to do it, is a good thing," Jesse said.

"And you'll stay?"

"I'll stay," Jesse said.

"What if I get to a point where what I want doesn't include you?"

"Then I'll move on," Jesse said.

"And you'll be all right?"

"Jenn, I don't know if I'm going to be all right tomorrow. I can't possibly tell you if I'll be all right in six months or two years or whatever it takes."

"But you won't give up?"

"Not until you tell that you don't want me in your life."

"I can't ever imagine saying that."

"That seems like good odds to me," Jesse said.

"The other night was good."

"Yes," Jesse said.

They were both quiet for a moment. Then she stood, Jesse opened his arms, Jenn stepped into them, and he held her hard. He could feel the completeness surge up inside him. There was no logic to it; he simply knew when he touched her that she was not like other women. He kept his arms around her, fighting off the desire to squeeze too hard, while she pressed her face against his chest and cried softly but not, Jesse thought, hopelessly.

chapter 49

"You got a safe-deposit box?" Macklin said.

The man was in designer sweat clothes that appeared as if they'd never been sweaty. His wife had on a tennis outfit, and she was standing rigidly still because Crow had the muzzle of the shotgun pushed up into the soft tissue under her chin. On the floor was a canvas duffel bag into which Macklin had dumped the cash and jewelry he had found.

"I . . ."

"You lie to me and your wife's brains will be decorating the ceiling," Macklin said.

He held his handgun casually in front of him, aimed more or less at the man's navel. The gun was cocked.

"I have one."

The man had iron-gray hair and a strong profile. He was the semi-retired CEO of something, and he was struggling to be brave and not succeeding. *You can be brave,* Macklin thought, *with a gun in your face, though it's easier* when there's no gun. But there's still nothing to do but what you're told.

"Paradise Bank?" Macklin said.

"Yes."

"Stiles Island branch?"

"Yes."

"Get the key."

The man hesitated. Macklin raised the handgun and placed the muzzle a half inch from the man's left eye.

"I'll count to three. Then your widow gets the key for us . . . One!"

"It's in my bureau drawer," the man said.

His voice wheezed out as if his throat was clogged with dust.

"I'll go with you," Macklin said, and he followed the man into the front hall and up the stairs.

"What are you going to do to us?" the woman said, her voice strained, her teeth clenched in parody of an upper-crust accent from the pressure of the shotgun.

"Nothing we don't have to," Crow said. "You got a downstairs lav?"

"Yes."

"Let's see it," Crow said and lowered the shotgun.

They walked to the front hall and back toward the kitchen. The woman indicated a door under the stairs next to the kitchen. Crow opened the door. It opened outward. He looked in. It was a big lavatory with a wash basin and makeup mirror and no windows.

Macklin came back down the stairs with the man. He held up the safe deposit key so that Crow could see it.

Crow nodded and jerked his head toward the lavatory.

"Here," Crow said. "Down this hall."

Macklin came down the hall and looked at the lavatory.

"Helps that these houses are all the same, don't it?" Macklin said. "Okay, both of you go into the lav and close the door and stay there."

The man and woman did as they were told. They're glad to, Macklin thought. Means we're not going to kill them. When the door was closed, Crow went to the living room and got the big gym bag. He came back down the hall and took a hammer and some 12D nails from the bag and nailed the lavatory door shut. Then he dropped the hammer back into the bag, put the shotgun in, picked the bag up, and he and Macklin, who was carrying the canvas duffel bag, walked out of the house. On the sidewalk, Macklin looked at his watch.

"Pretty good," he said. "We'll have them all by late afternoon."

"What's Fran telling people at the bridge?" Crow said. "What's that sign say?"

Macklin smiled.

"The sign says 'Caution: Blasting,' " he said. "Any civilians, Fran tells them the island's closed for a couple hours."

They walked up the manicured walkway of the next estate. Macklin rang the door bell and deep inside the house some chimes sounded. Macklin grinned at Crow.

"Avon calling," Macklin said and set his duffel bag down on the step beside him.

chapter 50

Abby Taylor lived in a weathered shingle home in the oldest part of Paradise. When she was married, she had bought it with her husband, and when they had divorced it remained with her. When her doorbell rang, she looked through the peephole in the front door and saw a well-dressed, good-looking, upper-class woman in her forties, who looked vaguely familiar. Abby opened the door.

"Hello," she said.

"Hello," the good-looking woman said and hit Abby flush on the jaw with her clenched right fist. It was a good punch, and it staggered Abby backward several steps. The woman stepped through the front door and closed it behind her. By the time Abby got her balance, the woman was aiming a .38 Smith & Wesson Chief's Special at her.

"What . . . the . . . Christ are you . . . doing?" Abby said. Her lip was already starting to puff.

"The punch was to get your attention," Faye said. She felt perfectly cold and steady inside. "If you don't do exactly what I say, I'll kill you. Do you believe that?"

Abby stared at her. It was hard to process anything. The woman slapped her hard across the face with her left hand.

"Do you believe that?" the woman said.

Abby nodded.

"Okay. We're going to go to your bedroom, and you're going to lie on the bed facedown. You got that? You so much as clear your throat, and I'll fill your head full of bullets."

"What are you going to do?" Abby said. Her voice sounded thin to her and puny.

"Anything I have to," the woman said. "You do what you're told, you'll get out of this alive. You don't, and you won't."

"Why?" Abby said. "Why are you doing this?"

The woman smiled without any hint of laughter.

"Love," she said.

"Love?"

The woman jerked her head toward the front stairs.

"Your bedroom up there?"

"Yes."

"Then move," the woman said.

As they went up the stairs, Abby could hear a dog bark somewhere and then someone whistling for it and then quiet. The quiet was oppressive. The house was thunderously empty except for her and this violent woman. They reached her bedroom.

"Lie on the bed," the woman said.

Abby did as she was told. The woman took a pair of handcuffs from her purse, and holding the gun in her right hand, she snapped one cuff on Abby's left wrist and the other to the headboard of the bed. Then she stepped back and put the gun in her purse and looked around the room. There was a phone on the bedside table. The woman unplugged it and put it in the hall. She looked out the window at Abby's backyard. The next house was fifty feet away. The window was closed. The woman lowered the window shade.

"Nobody can hear you," she said to Abby.

"What are you going to do to?"

"You'll be all right," the woman said. "It'll only be a while."

Then she shut the door and went downstairs, leaving Abby alone in the darkened bedroom.

chapter 51

Molly came into Jesse's office with two cups of coffee and a brown paper bag. She put a cup of coffee on his desk, took a raspberry turnover from the bag, handed it to him, and sat down opposite the desk.

"You busy," Molly said.

"Well, I was thinking of taking a ride to Charlestown again, see if I can find Harry Smith, aka James Macklin."

"The guy's a phony?"

"And a bad one."

"You going alone?"

"I thought I might bring a Boston detective with me."

"There's more going on here than I know about, isn't there?"

"Suit will fill you in. You make the turnover?"

"The Paradise Bake Shop helped me," Molly said.

"I got time to eat it," Jesse said.

Molly smiled.

"Figured you might like something soothing . . . or you can talk if you want," she said.

Jesse took the turnover out and had a bite. He chewed it while he pried the lid off the coffee cup.

"Don't need to talk," he said.

"Fine with me," Molly said. "Got a call from Citadel Security. They said the Stiles Island Patrol hadn't called in for a couple hours now. Asked us to check."

"Send somebody out?" Jesse said.

"Pat Sears and Billy Pope," Molly said.

"Good. There another turnover?"

Molly fumbled in the bag and took out a second turnover and handed it to him.

"Jenn didn't help things," Molly said.

"No."

"Kay Hopkins has a lot of say in this town," Molly said. "You'll have to take her seriously, Jesse."

"I do what I can do, Molly."

"I know, but Jenn assaulting her . . ."

"Jenn does what she can do."

"That's a funny situation," Molly said. "If you'll excuse my saying so. You're divorced, but you're not really separated."

"Yes, it's odd," Jesse said.

"Would you marry her again?" Molly said. "Tell me if I'm out of line."

"You're okay," Jesse said. "Yeah, I'd marry her again if I knew it would be monogamous."

"How could you know?"

"If she promised, I'd believe her."

Molly made a face.

"Your marriage monogamous?" Jesse said.

"Be no marriage if it weren't," Molly said.

"How do you know?"

"Because I'd leave in a heartbeat."

"No, I mean, how do you know your husband isn't cheating on you?"

"He wouldn't."

Jesse nodded. Molly frowned at him. Then she smiled. "You trust her?" Molly said.

"I trust her not to lie to me again."

"She lied to you before."

"Yes."

"So how can you know now that she wouldn't do it again?"

"Same way you do," Jesse said.

"But you have a history . . ."

"And when I was living that history, I knew I couldn't trust her. Now I know I can."

"And the other women? Abby? Marcy Campbell?"

"I'm a single guy," Jesse said. "I like women. I like sex with women."

"But you love Jenn."

"Yes."

"For me the two things sort of merge," Molly said.

"Love and sex?"

"Yes."

"You must be female," Jesse said.

"Irish Catholic female," Molly said. "The ultimate."

They were quiet for a moment.

"All of this is none of my business, is it?"

"No, it's not," Jesse said. "But it's nice to talk about it with someone who has no stake in the outcome."

"Well, I love you too, Jesse."

"Yeah, but not that way."

"No, I love my husband that way."

"Damn," Jesse said. And they both laughed.

chapter 52

As soon as JD cut the ropes, Marcy peeled off the duct tape that covered her mouth, picked up her purse without a word, and went into the small lavatory. She locked the door and used the lav, washed her hands and began to examine her face in the mirror. The tape had taken all her makeup and most of her lipstick with it. There was a big red mark across the lower part of her face where it had been. Marcy washed her face in the basin, and dried her face carefully. She didn't have enough makeup in her purse to repair the damage. All she could do was put on fresh lipstick and comb her hair. Then she stood silently with her forehead pressed against the mirror and her eyes closed. She felt safe in here, though she knew she wasn't. But she simply couldn't stay in here, cowering until what ever happened happened. She was better off than she had been. At least she wasn't tied up anymore. Harry and the Indian had told this man not to hurt her, and he seemed to do what they told him. If she had just given into impulse this morning and not come to work . . . that was pointless.

What was going to happen was what mattered. She took in
a deep breath and let it out and looked at herself in the mirror. *Okay, Marce, here you go.* She opened the lavatory
door and walked out into the office. JD was staring out the
office window at the guard shack and the bridge. He
glanced over his shoulder at her.

"Feeling better?" he said.

"Yes." Her voice was hoarse.

JD turned back toward the window.

"You need to stay in here and be quiet," he said. "I got
to concentrate. You give me a problem, and I'll kill you."

"Harry and the other man said I was not to be harmed."

"I know what they said. They meant if you were good.
You give any of us trouble, and any of us will kill you.
You understand?"

"Yes."

"You can't get off the island, and you can't make a
phone call, so sit down and relax and don't bother me."

"I won't bother you," Marcy said.

JD turned back to the window. Marcy glanced around
the office. She didn't want to sit on the couch where she
had lain so long tied up. She went and sat behind the desk.
It was, after all, her desk. If he wanted to sit there, he could
tell her. JD continued to stare out the window. His back
looked stiff. He was nervous. The office was very still. She
tried to breathe softly, looking at JD. He was a small man,
and he had about him a kind of skinny softness. It wasn't
fair. She was a big woman and strong. She worked out
every day at her health club. Yet this puny soft man was
stronger than she was and could force her to do what he
wanted. Of course, he had a gun. But even if he didn't, he
could overpower her. It didn't seem right. But that's how it
was. Clearly, God wasn't a woman.

"Can you tell me what's going on?" Marcy said.

JD shook his head.

"Well, what are you doing? Why are you all here?"

"Shhh!" JD said.

She felt a surge of anger. He was so dismissive. He
didn't even turn his head. All women felt that anger if they

let themselves. Though most women didn't find themselves, literally at least, in this kind of situation.

"For God's sake, you could at least look at me," Marcy
said.

JD turned slowly.

"You shut the fuck up, lady, or I'm going to come up
alongside of your fucking head."

She felt the thrill of fear run through her. He wasn't just
a sexist pig; he was a sexist pig with a gun, and she was his
prisoner. Remotely, almost unconnected with the reality
of her situation, the eternal footman of her consciousness
made an ironic little snicker. Her situation was probably
just a slightly intensified version of all women's situation,
the footman said. Everywoman!

"Jesus Christ," JD said.

Marcy stood behind the desk so she could look past him
out the window. A Paradise patrol car was driving across
the bridge. Marcy felt a surge of excitement. Help was
coming.

When the police car was halfway across, the bridge
began to ripple. The ripple turned into a heave. And, as
the sound of the explosion came rolling into the real estate
office, the bridge went up and the police car with it, som-
ersaulting slowly in among the pieces of the disintegrating
bridge. One of its doors blew away and the hood tore off,
and the car languidly turned over and planed into the gray
harbor and disappeared.

Marcy stood motionless, staring, as bridge debris continued to spin down and splash into the harbor. JD was for
a moment as transfixed as Marcy, watching the explosion
settle. Then he began punching numbers into his cell
phone.

"Jesus Christ," JD said. "Jesus Christ."

chapter 53

"Exploded?" Jesse said on the radio.

"Twenty calls at least," Molly said. "At least five people said there was a police car on the bridge when it went."

"You raise Pope and Sears?" Jesse said.

"No."

Jesse thought a minute. He was half-way to Boston, nearly to the dog track.

"Okay, everybody on the force is now on duty. Assemble them and stand by."

"Call the Staties?" Molly said.

"Let's see what we've got first," Jesse said.

He turned on the blue flasher, which he often did if he was in a hurry. He also turned on the siren, which he rarely did. He U-turned, bumping the car over the curbstone and listening to the protesting screech of the tires as he stepped hard on the accelerator pedal. In fifteen minutes, he was sitting in his idling car looking at the empty space above the water, where half of a steel girder dangling from the near abutment was all that remained. Some wreckage had washed against the near shore and bobbed against the rocks. There was no sign of the police car, not of Pope or Sears. Several cars full of sightseers had arrived, and some pedestrians had gathered as well.

Jesse got on the radio.

"Molly, the bridge is gone. Everybody there?"

"Everybody but Eddie Cox," Molly said. "His wife says he's out shopping. I left a message."

"Send a couple of guys down here to secure the place from the tourists. You hear from Pope and Sears?"

"Will do, Jesse. No response from Pope and Sears."

"Okay," Jesse said. "Send me two guys to secure this end of the bridge. Everyone else stand by at the station."

"Will do, Jesse. What do I tell Betty Pope and Kim Sears if they call?"

"Tell them what we know, Molly. Don't speculate. Tell them I see no sign of them, and you can't raise them on the radio, and people report a police car was on the bridge when it blew."

"That's going to be pretty hard to hear, Jesse."

"I know. Refer them to me if you'd rather."

"No, you got enough, Jesse. If they call, I'll talk with them. What happened?"

"Don't know. The only odd thing is there's maybe a dozen people down here already milling around looking at the wreckage."

"That's not odd," Molly said.

"Yeah. But there's no one at the other side. Not even the guy from the guard shack. Anything yet from the Stiles Island Patrol?"

"No. Want me to call the Staties yet?"

"You better, at least give them a heads up."

"Okay, Jesse. John and Arthur are on the way in a cruiser."

"Thanks, Molly. I'll get back to you."

Jesse sat back and thought about Wilson Cromartie, who preferred to be called Crow. And James Macklin of Dorchester, who had flirted with him not very long ago. He stared at the debris washed by the rough water against the near shore. And he knew, as if he'd seen them, that Macklin and Cromartie were on Stiles Island. It was what exactly he was supposed to do about it that still needed work.

chapter 54

The bank employees were herded into one corner of the vault, and half the safe deposit boxes had been opened when Macklin heard the bridge explode. He looked at Crow. Crow continued to take everything out of the open security box and dump it into his duffel bag. He dropped the key into the open box, took another key from his pocket and with the bank manager supplying the second key, opened the next box. Macklin's cell phone rang.

"Yeah."

"JD, Fran had to blow the bridge."

"I know, I heard it. It'll happen just like I said. They'll mill around for a while. Then they'll get a boat and come to the yacht club landing. When they get about halfway there, Fran will blow it."

"What do you want me to do?"

"What did I tell you to do, JD?"

"After Fran blows the boat landing, I call you and wait for instructions."

"Good, JD, you and Fran come to the bank. Help us load."

"Should we leave the bridge unguarded?"

"The bridge is gone, isn't it?"

"Yes."

"Then you don't need to guard it. And after Fran blows the boat landing, you won't need to guard it. Only way they can get to us is with a chopper, and it'll take some time for them to round one up. Am I going too fast for you, JD?"

"No, I'm just being careful."

"You were careful, you'd be down home drinking bourbon and Coca-Cola. Just do what I tell you."

"What do I do with the broad?" JD said.

"Leave her there, we got no need for her."

"Maybe we'll need a hostage," JD said.

Macklin smiled. "JD wonders if we need a hostage," Macklin said to Crow.

"Tell him not to think anymore," Crow said, without looking up from the lock boxes.

"Crow says don't think anymore," Macklin said.

"I was just . . . "

"JD, the whole fucking island is a hostage. We don't need to lug one around with us."

"Didn't you tell me she's the chief's girlfriend? It might help if we hung on to her."

"It might," Macklin said. "Go ahead and bring her." He broke the connection.

In the real estate office, JD stared at the silent cell phone.

"Prick," he said.

Marcy sat quietly behind her desk. Her hands folded on top of it. She could see that JD was tense. His movements were stiff and too quick. He stared out the window. Fran was walking back toward them from the wreckage of the bridge.

"Okay," JD said. "You're going with us."

"Where?" Marcy's voice rasped, and she cleared her throat. She'd heard JD's end of the conversation.

"Just get in the fucking car, lady. I got no time to explain things."

"I'm not really the chief's girlfriend," Marcy said. Her voice was still raspy. She couldn't seem to get it clear.

"You're fucking him, aren't you?"

Marcy didn't answer. JD gestured at her with his handgun.

"Come on," JD said. "Get in the car."

chapter 55

It was an overcast day, and the water in the harbor was darker than the sky. Jesse was onboard the town boat with Suitcase Simpson, Anthony DeAngelo, and Peter Perkins. Simpson, DeAngelo, and Perkins wore vests and carried shotguns. Jesse had neither. Phil Winslow, the harbor master, held the boat at an angle across the chop. steering for the yacht club landing dock that jutted out into the harbor.

"Only place I can put you ashore, Jesse," Winslow said. "The rest of the damn island is all rock and surf. I can't get within a hundred yards."

"Maybe they don't know that," Jesse said.

"No way they would unless they explored it," Winslow said. "Most people buy onto an island like this, they want beaches, you know? But Stiles Island uses the ocean like a Christly moat."

"It's working," Jesse said.

"Are you guys enough?" Winslow said.

"Have to be," Jesse said. "Don't have that many left.

Molly's at the station, Arthur and John Maguire are securing that end of the bridge, and I don't know where Eddie Cox is."

"Sears and Pope?" Winslow said.

"Probably dead," Jesse said.

"Jesus."

They were .in the middle of the harbor now, past the cluster of pleasure boats moored in closer to the dock. Winslow turned the boat north, running parallel with Paradise Neck, heading for Stiles Island. Sound traveled over water, and even this far from the scene Jesse could hear the sirens of the fire and emergency vehicles still arriving at the scene of the explosion, cops from neighboring towns, probably some state cops. Molly would get them organized.

Ahead of them Jesse could see the fanciful cornices of the yacht club, white and pink, with a playful balcony across the second floor and a high-peaked red roof. Stiles Island people were very proud of it. Jesse thought it looked like an eighty-dollar-a-night motel in Flagstaff. The landing dock was actually a kind of catwalk set on pilings that went out nearly the length of a football field into the harbor. At the end of the catwalk, down a short flight of stairs, was a wide float anchored to the bottom and tethered to the catwalk pilings. There was enough play in the anchor chains so that the float rolled gently with the movement of the harbor. There was a resting bottom up on the float. No one was in sight. Winslow aimed the nose of the town boat straight at the float. As Jesse watched, the float began to heave and then it and the catwalk elevated as the sound of the explosion rolled across the water to them. The float turned over twice in midair. The empty drums that helped it float tore loose and scattered across the water. The catwalk disintegrated in midair, and the pieces seemed to hang there, as the float drifted down and landed bottom side up in the suddenly frantic water. The town boat pitched as the waves reached it, and Winslow wrestled the wheel around to stay stable. The silence after the explosion seemed louder than silence could be. It was underscored but not dispelled by the sound of the boat engine and the nowturbulent ocean slapping against the hull. Winslow throttled back and held the boat sideways, idling, in the deep swells. No one spoke for a moment.

Then Jesse said, "Bad guys two, cops zip."

Winslow said, "What do you want me to do now, Jesse?"

"You know anyplace else to land?"

"No."

"Who would?"

Winslow shrugged.

"Maybe there ain't a place," he said.

"There'll be a place. Who knows the harbor better than you?"

"Can't say anybody does," Winslow said.

"Then let's go back to town," Jesse said.

The boat made a wide turn, and Winslow throttled up for the run back to the town wharf.

Suitcase said, "Usually get three strikes, don't you, Jesse?"

"At least," Jesse said.

chapter 56

"Ladies and gentlemen," Macklin said, holding the 9-mm almost negligently at his side, "as you no doubt have figured, the shit has hit the fan, and it is time for us to go. We thank you for your patience, and your valuables."

The bank employees stood silent, standing close together as if for warmth. Behind him, Fran was carrying the last duffel bag out of the vault toward the stairs to the street where JD held the van with its motor running.

"Okay," Macklin said. "We need some hostages for a while."

He looked at Crow. "Gimme five women. They're less trouble."

Crow moved in among the employees and cut out the five hostages. They moved numbly, not knowing what else to do.

"We won't need them for too long," Macklin said. "We'll let them go when we leave. The rest of you want to run around after we've left and free some of your friends and neighbors," Macklin said, "go right ahead."

He grinned and scanned them.

"Any questions?"

No one spoke.

"Hasta la vista."

He turned and nodded at Crow and the two of them walked from the vault. No one in the vault moved. Macklin and Crow walked upstairs and through the empty bank, moving the women before them the way dogs move sheep. Crow's van was parked at the bank entrance right behind Macklin's Mercedes. JD and Fran were leaning on the van. Both had shotguns, and both men had a pinched look to their faces. Marcy was sitting on the floor in the back of the van. Crow herded the five women into the back of the van with her.

"What are they for?" JD said.

"Hostages," Macklin said.

"We already got her," JD said, nodding at Marcy.

"Can't have too many," Macklin said.

In the back of the van, crouched on the floor among the loaded duffel bags, a very young plump woman with a lot of frizzy blond hair began to cry. An older woman with gray hair in a tight perm, and horn-rimmed glasses on a strap around her neck, put her arm around the young woman and patted her shoulder. Marcy watched silently. *You'll get used to it,* she thought. She was, after all, a veteran hostage. She had several hours experience on these women.

"It's going to be all right," the older woman said. "It's going to be fine."

Maybe, Marcy thought, *and maybe not.* Macklin looked at JD and Fran.

"Are we having fun yet?" he said.

"How long you think, Jimmy, before the cops get here?" Fran said.

"Long as it takes to get a big chopper up here and put a SWAT team on it."

"What if they do it quick?" Fran said.

"That's why God made hostages," Macklin said.

He looked at the Mercedes.

"Got to leave you here, old buddy," he said to the car. "Good-bye."

He raised the 9-mm and turned his head away as if in grief and shot through the hood of the car. He laughed loudly. Fran glanced at Crow. Crow's face showed nothing.

"Come on," JD said. "Let's get to the boat."

Macklin looked at his watch.

"We're too quick," he said. "Got four hours still to high tide."

"We got to sit here and wait four hours?" Fran said.

"Sit someplace," Macklin said. "You feel better sitting by the rendezvous, fine with me."

"So let's go," Fran said. "Stop standing here out in the open."

Macklin looked at Crow and said, "These boys just haven't learned how to have fun."

"Scared," Crow said.

"No pain, no gain," Macklin said.

Crow nodded and laid the shotgun crossways on the dashboard and got in behind the wheel. JD and Fran scrambled into the backseat and Macklin, after a last look around, like a tourist leaving a favorite resort, climbed into the passenger seat and closed the door. The women crouched in the cargo space behind them. The one who had been crying was silent now.

"How much you think we got?" JD said, as the van moved along the empty street.

"The houses? The retail stores? The bank? The safe deposit boxes?" Macklin said. "Six, eight million maybe? Whaddya think, Crow?"

"I think we need to count it when we got time," Crow said.

"What if Freddie's not there?" Fran said.

"He'll be there," Macklin said. "Freddie always does what he says. It's what makes him such a bad hard-on."

Macklin was drumming his fingertips lightly on the tops of his thighs. His eyes were bright and seemed to be opened wider than normal. His toes tapped the floorboards of the van in time with his fingertips.

"But what if he's not?" Fran said.

Macklin shifted a little in the seat so he could look straight at Fran.

"Fran, we just pulled off the mother fucker of all heists, you understand? This is a time to be cool and feel it and kick back and like it. This ain't a time to be whining."

"Fran's got four kids," Crow said.

"Shoulda thought about that when I invited him in," Macklin said.

"I did," Fran said.

"Then shut the fuck up," Macklin said.

"You don't have to talk to me that way, Jimmy," Fran said.

"I'll talk to you anyway I want," Macklin said.

"Got to understand," Crow said gently. "Jimmy isn't doing this for the money. That's just the way he keeps score."

"You don't have to talk for me, Crow," Macklin said.

"The real thing he does it for is this, the charge, the danger, the goose it gives him, you understand? He does it same reason people do downhill skiing or sky diving. This is like getting laid for Jimmy, and right now when he's just ready to come, you're spoiling the feeling."

"What the fuck are you, Doctor Spock?" Macklin said.

Crow paid no attention to him.

"We'll pull this off or we won't," Crow said. "And worrying out loud about it ain't going to do you any good, and it's going to piss Jimmy off really bad."

"And that won't do you any fucking good either," Macklin said.

Crow didn't say anything else. Fran was silent and so was JD. Macklin resumed his finger drumming and toe tapping as they left the little downtown and swung onto Sea Street.

chapter 57

When Jesse walked into the station with Simpson, DeAngelo, and Perkins, Molly was working the switchboard and covering the front desk.

"There's a guy from the Coast Guard on his way, Jesse," Molly said as he walked in, "and a State Police SWAT guy in your office."

Jesse said, "Thank you, Molly. Anthony, go find Doc Lane and bring him here."

"The bartender at the Gull?"

"Yep. If he's not working, ask the restaurant for his address. Peter, go find me a wet suit, medium. And some kind of waterproof equipment flotation. If you can't find anything closer, there's a place in Belmont on Trapelo Road."

"Flotation?"

"Yes. Go. Get it. Bring it back. Now."

Perkins and DeAngelo left the station. Suitcase stayed with Jesse waiting to be told what to do. Jesse nodded toward his office, and they went in.

The SWAT team commander was a lean guy with round glasses and a crew cut. He put out a hand.

"Ray Danforth," he said.

"Jesse Stone. The big kid here is Suitcase Simpson."

"Lighter color than I remember you," Danforth said.

Suitcase looked blank. Danforth turned to Jesse.

"I got my men standing by at the explosion site," Danforth said. "We got a mobile operations van on the way. What can you tell me?"

"What I know is that somebody blew the bridge to Stiles Island. Somebody also blew the landing dock at the yacht club on Stiles. No one has heard from the Stiles Island Security patrol since last night, and all the phones on Stiles give a busy signal when you call them."

"What do you guess?"

"A guy named Wilson Cromartie and a guy named James Macklin and probably some others are on the island. I assume the motive is robbery."

"How they going to get off the island?"

"Don't know."

"People on the island?"

"Far as I know, about a hundred."

"I'll get a hostage negotiator up here," Danforth said.

"Good. Let's not get any civilians killed," Jesse said.

"We got a traffic helicopter should be here anytime," Danforth said. "And a transport chopper if we need one. That'll take a little longer. We got to fly it in from Hanscomb Field."

"Better call it up. We don't want to have to wait for it when we need it."

"Will do," Danforth said. "What's your plan?"

"I might go ashore."

"Alone?"

"Yeah. Might be a good idea to have someone on the ground."

"Police chiefs don't usually do that kind of work," Danforth said.

"This is a small-town department," Jesse said. "It's sort of informal here. We all pitch in."

"You don't have anyone else you'd trust?" Danforth said. "Or you don't want to ask anyone else?"

Jesse shrugged.

"Whatever," he said.

"Who's going to run the department?"

"Molly," Jesse said, "and Suit." He nodded at Simpson.

"I ought to come with you, Jesse," Suitcase said.

"You stay here. Molly shouldn't have to run it alone."

"You remember what that cop said in Tucson," Suitcase said.

"I'm not going up against anyone," Jesse said. "I'm just reconnaissance, you know? I'm just going to scoot around in the bushes and see what I can see and radio it back."

"I could cover your back," Suit said.

"You're too big to scoot around in the bushes," Jesse said. "You go with Lieutenant Danforth. Molly will stand by in the station, and I will have a look see on the island."

"How you going to get there?" Suitcase said.

"I'm working on that."

"Doc?"

"He's been around this harbor all his life," Jesse said.

"You going to have him put you in the water?"

"Probably," Jesse said.

"And?" Suit said.

"And we'll see," Jesse said.

chapter 58

The helicopter came up from the southeast, across the causeway to Paradise Neck and then across the harbor. It hovered for a time over the explosion site, then banked suddenly and flew down the Stiles Island coast and paused again, this time over the boat house explosion.

It moved away from the yacht club and began unhurriedly to fly back and forth over Stiles Island, looking at what there was to look at. Across the empty span where the bridge had hung, there was a gathering of trucks and automobiles and people. The helicopter paused again over the small downtown where people were gathered in the street, looking up, then moved on toward the open ocean side of the island where the restaurant was located.

In the van, Crow heard the helicopter first and glanced up through the van window. It wasn't in sight yet. As the van pulled up beside the restaurant, they all heard it.

"Chopper," Fran said.

Macklin looked up through the van window and watched the helicopter come in over the treetops and hover over them. Then he got out of the van and walked around to the back and opened the doors.

"Everybody out," he said, and the six women climbed out and stood silently beside the van.

The helicopter dropped down a little and Macklin fired four rounds from his handgun at it. The helicopter heeled sharply and soared in the same motion and was out of range almost at once.

"Let 'em know we're here," Macklin said.

"I think they know that," Crow said.

"They're going to know it even more in a minute," Macklin said. "JD, gimme the cell phone."

Five hundred yards offshore, holding the boat steady against the rough chop, Freddie Costa watched the helicopter fly back across the island, out of pistol range. The prow of the boat pounded steadily as the short waves pushed at it. He looked at his watch. Three and a half hours.

Across the island, across Stiles Island gut, where the roiling water foamed over the wreckage of the bridge on the Paradise side, in the mobile operations command truck, a radio operator talked with the helicopter pilot. Ray Danforth stood listening. Suitcase Simpson was with him, looking a little uncomfortable among the State SWAT team cops with their black fatigues and their assault weapons and their funky gun belts.

"I think the bandits are at the restaurant on the open ocean side of the island. We drew some small arms fire," the pilot said. "There's a power boat maybe four, five hundred yards offshore. From here, it doesn't look like he can get closer."

"Okay," Danforth said to the radio operator. "Tell them to stay out of range but monitor."

He turned to Suitcase.

"When is high tide around here?"

"Don't know," Suitcase said, "but I'll find out."

"Do that," Danforth said.

chapter 59

"Lemme call Carleton Jencks," Doc said.

"Snapper's father?"

"Yeah. He knows the harbor better than I do."

The phone rang.

"Okay. Have Molly call him from the switchboard," Jesse said and picked up the phone.

"This is Harry Smith," the voice said.

Doc went out to the desk.

"Or James Macklin," Jesse said. It could have been Cromartie, but the voice didn't have that indefinable Indian overtone that Jesse remembered from his childhood.

There was silence on the phone for a moment, and then Macklin went on.

"I'm on the island. And I wanted to run couple things by you. First, the next helicopter I see anywhere around here, I shoot a hostage."

"Uh-huh."

"Second, any boats, anything, any attempt to land on the island, any interference with us as we go about our business, and I shoot hostages. I got a lot of them. I can shoot a bunch and have plenty left."

"What business are you going about?" Jesse said.

"Our business," Macklin said.

"And when will you be through going about it?"

"I'll let you know," Macklin said. "Remember what I told you. I see so much as a fucking sea scallop come ashore, and it'll be a blood bath."

"We don't want that," Jesse said.

"No you don't, and if I see you out here, I'll go shoot that broad you been fucking."

"Which one?" Jesse said and winced silently as he heard the way it sounded.

"Way to go, Stone," Macklin said. "Marcy, the real estate lady."

"Uh-huh."

"You fuck up, and she goes first."

Jesse took in air silently and flexed his shoulders, forcing himself to relax. "I hear you," Jesse said.

"Got anything to say?"

"We'll cooperate," Jesse said. "You've got my word on it."

"Well, isn't that good," Macklin said.

He turned off the cell phone and put it on the bar in the empty restaurant where they were holding the hostages. Marcy sat on a bar stool at the other end of the bar looking at the floor.

"Says he'll cooperate," Macklin said. "Guess he don't want you to get hurt, Marcy."

Marcy didn't say anything.

"I mentioned the woman he'd been fucking, and he asked me which one," Macklin said and put his head back and laughed. It was a loud laugh and long and, Marcy thought, somehow contrived, just as it was contrived the way he threw his head back. He was posturing.

"Where's JD and Fran?" Macklin said to Crow.

"Guard duty," Crow said, "I told them to go out and walk around the building, keep an eye out."

"Good, serves a useful purpose and keeps them from

whining at me. This thing is going down so good there's not enough O's in smooth."

Crow nodded and glanced out the window at the water that boiled through the offshore rocks as the tide came slowly in. Freddie was out of sight around the low headland to the right. Crow glanced at his watch.

Carleton Jencks came into the office with Snapper.

"I brought my son," Jencks said.

"Can you get me ashore on Stiles?"

Jencks nodded slowly.

"Got to bring Snapper, though. He's the one knows."

"Too dangerous to bring a kid."

"He's got to show us," Jencks said.

"He can tell us."

Jencks shook his head. "Not enough margin for error," he said. "Place is about five feet wide."

"You know how to get ashore on Stiles?" Jesse said to Snapper.

"Yeah."

"Answer right," Carleton Jencks said.

"Yes," Snapper said. "Yes sir, I do."

"Tell me."

"It's on the harbor side, about halfway between the yacht club and the bridge. Me and some other guys used to go over there in my father's rowboat. Anchor it and swim ashore, watch what went on."

Maybe steal a little something too, Jesse thought. But he had bigger things to worry about, and he dismissed the thought.

"Can you tell me how to go in?"

"Not really . . . sir . . . I got to show you. There's no real landmarks, you know?"

Jesse sighed. He had no choice.

"Okay," he said. "You and your father."

He looked at Jencks. "You know how to use a gun?"

"Yes."

"You want one?"

"Got one," Jencks said.

Not the time to ask him for his permit, Jesse thought.

"I got a shotgun on the boat," Doc said.

"Okay," Jesse said, "here's the deal. Doc, you take us. Snapper tells us where. I'll go in alone."

"Before me and my kid sign on here, we need to know what's going on."

"You do," Jesse said and told them what he knew.

"High tide will be in about three hours," Doc said to Jesse.

"Okay," Jesse said. "I figure that's how long we got. Chopper pilot says there's a boat lingering on the ocean side of the island. My guess is it can get in close enough at high tide to take them off."

"Near the restaurant?" Jencks said.

"Yes. You think?"

"Yeah. It gets to where you can get in about twenty yards offshore and it's shallow enough to wade out."

"We let them get on the boat with the hostages, and we have a hairball," Jesse said.

"Like you don't have one now?" Doc said.

"Now we've got room to maneuver," Jesse said. "Bad guys and hostages on a small boat in the open sea . . . ?" Jesse shook his head.

"You figure they're over on the other side, by the restaurant?" Jencks said.

"Yes," Jesse said. "That's where they were when they fired on the chopper."

"You don't want to go ashore there."

"No."

"Then we'll have to put you ashore where Snapper says."

"Can you swim?" Jencks asked.

"Yes."

"Good?" Doc asked him.

"Good enough."

"I hope so," Doc said.

chapter 60

Marcy knew all of the hostages. Stiles Island was small, and those who worked there had a silent mutual contempt for those who lived there. The young blond woman who had been crying was Patty Moore. She was twenty-two and worked as a teller in the bank. The gray-haired woman who had comforted her was Agnes Till, the assistant manager. Patty was single, lived with her divorced mother in Paradise. Agnes was married with three grown children. She commuted to Stiles Island every day from Danvers. Judy, Mary Lou, and Pam were all tellers, all young, all white. Judy and Pam were married and childless. Mary Lou was a lesbian, though most people, including the Paradise Bank, didn't know it. She had spoken of it to Marcy once last spring at this bar on a Friday night after three Long Island iced teas. There were no black people on Stiles Island, residents or workers.

All of the women sat at two tables pushed together in the corner of the empty restaurant. They didn't talk. There was nothing to say. Patty Moore's eyes were still damp, but she had herself under enough control to be quiet. Marcy stared out the window and watched the early evening begin to darken the surface of the ocean.

Macklin was behind the bar. He took a shaker from under the bar and made some martinis. He held the shaker up.

"Crow?"

Crow shook his head.

"Ladies?"

No one answered. Macklin shook his head.

"Fine," he said. "More for me."

He poured the martini through the spring strainer into a martini glass, rummaged under the bar, found a jar of olives, and added three to his drink. Then he raised it toward the group of women sitting close together and took a drink.

"Ahhh," he said.

His movements were too quick, Marcy thought. And his jolliness was too forced, and there was something wrong with him. He'd been so calm when he'd come to the office and tied her up. He'd been— she thought about the right word — he'd been so contented when he'd arrived. Despite being his captive, or maybe because of it, she'd had a certain confidence in him to make this come out all right. Now he frightened her. She looked at Crow. He was unchanged. He was neither calm nor excited, not fast not slow, not kind not cruel. He seemed simply to be who he was.

Crow met her look.

"You're worried about Jimmy," he said.

She didn't answer.

"The fun part is over now for Jimmy," Crow said as if Macklin weren't there. "All the planning, putting together the crew, thinking about it, doing it! It's what Jimmy lives for."

"What am I?" Macklin said. "A fucking Lally column?"

"You know this is true, Jim," Crow said. "You get to this point, job's done. All you got to do now is get out with the dough. And they might still get you before you do."

Crow turned his attention back to Marcy.

"That's what keeps him from crashing."

"Hey, Crow, maybe you could stop talking about me like I'm a fucking nut case? I know you're bad, but I'm sort of bad myself and you're starting to piss me off."

Crow smiled at Marcy.

"See?" he said. "He's a danger freak."

Marcy didn't say anything. She didn't dare.

"You think I'm afraid of you, Crow?" Macklin said.

"This will go better, Jimmy," Crow said, "we don't get to shooting at each other."

Macklin poured himself another martini. "You make-um heap good point," Macklin said and smiled widely at Marcy. "Smart Indian, huh Marce?"

Marcy nodded very slightly, trying to be noncommittal.

"You ladies sure you won't drink something? Loosen up. You got to be here awhile, no reason not to enjoy it."

The frizzy-haired blond girl said, "I could have some white wine if you got some."

"Sure thing, blondie," Macklin said. "Step right up here."

Still behind the bar, Macklin reached down and got a wine glass and set it on the bar. He took a bottle of California Chardonnay from the refrigerator and pulled the cork and poured the glass three quarters full.

"There you are, blondie."

Marcy knew the girl wished she hadn't asked. She hadn't realized she'd have to walk up there and get it. Separation from the group seemed frightening. She would, Marcy knew, feel isolated at the bar.

"I'll have a little wine," Marcy said.

It was as if she was listening to someone else's voice.

"That's the spirit, Marce," Macklin said.

She and Patty stood and walked together to the bar and took their wine.

"Stay here," Macklin said.

For a moment, the false jollity was gone. It wasn't an invitation. It was an order. Which was how they understood it. Macklin raised his glass.

"Success," he said.

The two women raised theirs and drank. Marcy was grateful for the thrust of the wine. Even one sip made almost immediate contact with the electrical charge of her fear, and she felt it pulse through her. She took another quick drink. Macklin noticed. The bastard seemed to notice everything.

"Hits the spot," Macklin said.

"Happy hour," Crow said.

"Feel free to join us," Macklin said.

Crow shook his head.

"I think I'll go check the perimeter," he said.

"Nobody's gonna do squat while we got these women," Macklin said. "Hell, we got a hundred more back in town, we use these up."

"Nice to have bench strength," Crow said.

Macklin looked at his watch.

"Getting on," he said. "Crow, I think it's time for you to go out and see JD and Fran."

"There's a lot of stuff to be carried to the boat," Crow said. "Maybe better to wait."

Macklin smiled.

"These ladies will help us," he said. "Go ahead."

Crow nodded and went.

chapter 61

Jesse went into the water wearing a black neoprene wet suit and trailing a buoyant equipment bag. There was a Browning 9-mm in the bag and a .38 Smith & Wesson Chief's Special and a sunbelt. There was also a towel, a police radio, a fourbattery Maglite, and a change of clothes. He was a hundred yards offshore on the harbor side of the island, opposite the point on the ocean side where Macklin was holding the hostages. The water was cold, but the wet suit made it tolerable. The shore ahead of him was only a thicker darkness outlined against a paler sky. Above the dark silence of the powerless island, a crescent moon hung faint against the not yet fully gathered darkness. Doc had cut the engines and coasted in as close as he dared. Now he was letting the boat drift away before starting up the engines.

The rising tide made it easy to swim toward shore. Jesse looked back. He couldn't see the boat. The water was rougher as he got closer to shore, and the waves began to toss him among the rocks. He maneuvered through them by pushing himself away from them. The rocks were slick with seaweed and rough with barnacles. He couldn't touch bottom yet. A clump of seaweed brushed his leg, and he felt the panic he'd always felt when he was over his head. It wasn't drowning. He was terrified of sharks or, even more namelessly, of whatever might be lurking down there in the unfathomable space below, rising slowly toward his disembodied legs dangling against the surface of the water like bait. He felt the frantic impulse for a moment to climb up onto one of the rocks and cling there in useless safety. He took in a deep breath and let it out slowly. *In,* he said to himself as he breathed, *out.* Be a nice headline. POLICE CHIEF HIDES ON ROCK AS BANDITS LOOT ISLAND. He kept moving, breathing deeply, talking to himself, repelling gently from rock to rock, trying not to bang hard against one. *If there's something down there, it won't know I'm a cop. There hasn't been a shark fatality in Massachusetts since 1938.* Then he felt bottom and in another moment was able to stand. Still under pressure from the waves, he moved among the rock scatter closer to shore until he reached a sort of V-shaped gully in the rocks, where the seawater churned into a creamy foam. He scrambled up the gully and out of the ocean. At the top of the gully was some scrub pine, and he used it to climb the final few feet onto level ground. He was in a grove of white pine maybe a half mile farther out on the island from the yacht club. He knew where he was. He and Doc had planned for him to come out there because it would shelter him.

He stripped off the wet suit, toweled himself dry, shivering. It was too late in September to be standing naked at the edge of the water at night. He put on sneakers and jeans and a dark blue tee shirt. He strapped his gun belt on, with the Browning behind his right hip, and the .38 butt forward in front of his left. He clipped on the radio. There were two extra magazines for the Browning on the belt and a metal loop for the flashlight. He put on a blue windbreaker with gray Polartec lining and turned up the collar. The warmth was heartening. He clipped the radio mike to the collar. He took out of the flotation bag a zipper sandwich bag full of .38 special ammunition, stuck it in the side pocket of the windbreaker, and zipped the pocket. He rolled up the wet suit and the flotation bag and tossed them down into the surf at the foot of the rock gully. Then he turned and shrugged his shoulders to loosen them and shook his wrists and breathed deeply like a method actor before a scene.

Jesse looked at the roadway, thirty yards from the pine grove. There were no street lights. There was no electricity on the island since the bridge blew. The bank had its own generator, so that no one could get trapped in the vault by a power failure. But he wasn't anywhere near the bank, and he was pretty sure that light wasn't his friend anyway. If he followed that road for maybe two miles he would reach the restaurant on the other side where the chopper had taken fire. He breathed deep again. *In. Out. In. Out.* He thought about Marcy. He worked on his breathing. *In. Out. In. Out.* There was no movement on the roadway. No sound in the pine grove except the sound his heart made pumping too fast. The crescent moon had gone a little higher above the horizon. The sky was a little darker.

Okay, he thought, *here we go.*

suitcase simpson thought it looked like there was a festival at the Paradise end of the ruined bridge. Five television trucks were jammed in as close as the police would let them, their funny-looking antennas sticking up like the dead limbs of an old evergreen. Five television news people, three male and two female, were fighting for stand-up space in front of the wreckage, while their camera men were jostling each other for a better angle on the twisted ruins of the bridge, and the sound people were trying to get enough ambient noise for authenticity without drowning out the news person. There was a high volume of crowd hubbub. And the surf rolling up on the bare rocks was loud.

All three Paradise Police cruisers were parked near the verge of the channel, and half a dozen blue and gray State Police cruisers were scattered behind them. A big State Police mobile operations van sat in the middle of the roadway back of the cars with antennas sticking out of it variously. Both the Paradise fire trucks were there, along

with the town ambulance. There were fire trucks and
ambulances from three other towns, the crews sitting on
their trucks staring at the place where the bridge had
been. And there were a number of smaller vans with radio
call letters on the sides parked back along the roadway.
Much of Paradise was gathered behind the sawhorse bar-
ricades, and yellow crime scene tape stretched across the
operations scene. A lot of them had Walkman-type radios
with ear phones and were listening to the description
being broadcast by the half dozen radio reporters, who
were less ostentatious than the TV guys.

Suitcase was walking the perimeter of what he thought
of, for lack of something more descriptive, as the crime
scene. There was no reason to walk it. But he didn't know
what else to do. Danforth, the SWAT team guy, was in
considerable charge in the mobile unit, and some lieutenant commander from the Coast Guard had shown up
wearing a pistol belt and side arm and talking about a cut-
ter on the way from Boston. There were several technician
types working the radio and phones and a computer that
Suitcase didn't see the need for, and it was crowded, so he
took a walk. He could make sure the crowd didn't push
through the barriers and get in the way. Might as well do
something.

"Suit, what happened?"

"Bridge blew up."

"I can see that, for crissake."

"So what are you asking me for?"

"Suit, anyone killed?"

"Too soon to know."

Two guys he played softball with were sitting in a Ford
150, drinking beer.

"Hey, Suit, looks like a long day, babe. Want one?"

Suitcase shook his head. "Keep the cans in the
truck," he said.

He felt bad that Jesse hadn't taken him when he went to
the island. And he was very relieved that he didn't have to
go. Which made him more unhappy because it made him
question his courage. In the distance, he could hear more

sirens. He wondered what other vehicle could possibly be arriving in a great hurry to sit and wait. He saw the Hopkins boys smirking and jostling on a rock outcropping near the edge of the water. *Too bad they weren't on the fucking bridge when it went.* He tried to call Molly Crane on his radio and got the fire dispatcher.

"She ain't here," the dispatcher said. "She told me to take her calls."

"Where'd she go?"

"I don't know, but she was wearing a vest and she was in a big rush."

"Shit," Suitcase said.

"What's happening down there, Suit?"

"I got no idea," Suitcase said.

It was fully dark now. Inside the restaurant, Macklin had lit some candles. Outside, the only light was the small moon, which made thin bright traces on the dark water. Crow thought he could make out the shape of Freddie Costa's boat lingering out past the little jut of rock to his right, but it was only an area of thicker darkness and he wasn't sure. It was forty-eight minutes until Freddie could get in close enough. Crow turned and found JD standing near the back door of the restaurant, holding his shotgun.

"It's me, JD," Crow said as he walked toward him.

"How much time?"

" 'Bout three quarters of an hour," Crow said.

"This is fucking spooky," JD said. "I mean here we are, and they know we're here and nobody's doing nothing about it, and we're just hanging around."

"Cops can't get in touch with us," Crow said. "Jimmy didn't give them his cell phone number. They don't dare fly over because of the hostages."

"You don't think they got boats? Out a ways where we can't see them?"

"This ain't the FBI, JD. This is a small-town police department."

"You don't think the state cops will show up? You don't think they'll bring in the Coast Guard?"

"Sooner or later," Crow said. He was watching the darkness as he talked.

"And then what?"

"Then we got the hostages."

"You think we can pull this off, Crow?"

"Sure."

"So why am I so worried, and you're not?"

Crow smiled in the darkness.

"Well, aside from me being me, and you being you—you got to trust the team. You got to trust Freddie to get in here and pick us up and get us out of here, even if they got a boat out there looking for us. You got to trust me to handle trouble if it comes, and Jimmy to think this through."

"Jimmy's fucking crazy," JD said. "He was great before this thing started to go down. Now he's fucking coming apart."

"Still got to trust him. He's in charge. You unnerstand? We trusted you on the wiring. We trusted Fran on the boom. Now you got to trust us. Nobody's any good alone. You trust yourself. You trust your crew."

"Why didn't Jimmy time this closer?" JD said. "Waiting like this is weird."

Crow took a Bowie knife from the back of his belt and held it up so JD could look at it.

"You take a good knife," Crow said. "You need to grind the edge of it regular, or it gets dull."

"What's that?" JD said. "A fucking Apache slogan or something?"

"Or something," Crow said.

With a movement so quick that JD never saw it, he cut JD's throat, moving sideways as he did so to avoid the blood. A sigh of escaping air was the only sound JD made before he fell forward facedown on the ground and jerked briefly, like a slaughtered chicken, and was still. Crow put the knife blade into the earth a couple of times to clean it and then wiped the dirt off on his pants leg. He put the knife back and took out his gun.

"Fran," he yelled.

"Yo."

"Get over here."

Crow could hear Fran's footsteps as he came on the run. When he came around the corner, Crow shot him in the chest three times. The bullets spun Fran several staggering steps sideways, and the shotgun he had been carrying sailed off into the darkness. Fran fell on his back on top of JD.

Without looking at the dead men, Crow uncocked the pistol, dropped the magazine from the handle, and put the gun back in its holster. He took some loose ammunition from his pocket and fed three fresh rounds into the magazine. Then he took the gun back out, slid the magazine back into the handle, and holstered the gun again. He paid no attention to the two bodies lying together in the weak moonlight. He looked again out at the water and then walked down to the edge of it where it slid tamely over the stony beach.

He could see Freddie's boat now. It had moved past the rock jut and followed the tide in. It was still beyond the boulder that marked the farthest point they could wade. Crow turned and walked back into the restaurant. Macklin looked at him as he came into the romantic glow of candle light. Crow held up two fingers. Macklin nodded and smiled and turned to the hostages.

"Not to worry, ladies, just a little downsizing," he said.

chapter 64

Molly Crane was alone at the desk when the call came in. She automatically registered the phone number that flashed up on the caller ID screen.

"Chief Stone, please," a woman's voice said.

"He's not here," Molly said. "This is Sergeant Crane. May I help you?"

"Where is he?"

"Official business," Molly said. "May I have your name, please?"

"Tell Chief Stone that if he ever wants to see his sweetheart alive, he'll make sure that nothing happens to Jimmy Macklin."

"And what sweetheart might that be?" Molly said.

As she talked, she was punching up the phone number index on the computer.

"Abby Taylor," the voice said. "Anything happens to Jimmy Macklin, she dies."

"Would you like to make some sort of a deal?" Molly said.

"You let Jimmy go. I let Abby go."

The phone number came up on the screen. The woman was calling from Abby's phone. That was pretty brazen.

"May I speak with Abby, please?"

"And don't try to find me. I see a cop, and I'll kill her anyway."

"How do I know she's all right?" Molly said.

The woman didn't answer and the connection broke.

"Shit," Molly said aloud.

Was she really staying right in Abby's house? She called the mobile operations truck at the bridge. No answer. She shook her head once, then left the switchboard, went to her locker, and slipped into a bullet-proof vest. Then she went next door to the fire station.

Buzz Morrow was the only fireman there. Everyone else was at the explosion site.

"I'm leaving the station," she said. "Can you cover the switchboard?"

"I'm supposed to stand by here," Buzz said.

"You got no trucks," Molly said. "What happens if someone does report a fire? You run out and pee on it?"

"Good point," Buzz said. "Where you going?"

She didn't answer him. She left the fire station at a half run and went to the parking lot behind the station. There were no squad cars. She stopped at her own car, a Honda Accord, took out her service pistol and racked a 9-mm cartridge up into the chamber. She let the hammer back down, put the pistol back in its holster, took a deep breath, and got in her car. She had no siren, but the town was nearly deserted and she was able to go very fast through the empty streets. She went past Abby's street slowly and looked down it. Nothing unusual. No car in front of Abby's house. She turned the corner on the next street and circled the block slowly, staying off Abby's street. Nothing unusual. She saw a dark green Mercedes sedan near the corner. But Mercedes sedans were not unusual in Paradise. She parked on the street behind and a little bit downhill from Abby's house. Her breath was shallow and coming very fast. When she shut off the engine, she tried to slow down, relax the stomach muscles, breathe in deeply. She let her shoulders sag and closed her eyes for a minute.

Okay, okay. You're a cop, just like the other guys. You always knew you might have to do this. The fucking truth is, though, you always thought you'd be doing this with a couple of the guys.

She shook her head as if to clear it and got out of her car. She locked it and put the keys in the pocket of her uniform pants. Her pistol belt felt heavy. She hitched it higher. There was a radio on her belt and a can of Mace and some handcuffs and two extra magazines for her service pistol. The loop for the flashlight was empty. She didn't have a come along. Or a night stick. She had a short leather sap in her right-hand back pocket. From the trunk of her Honda, she took the jack handle and carried it in her left hand.

Okay, she thought again. *Okay.*

She walked quietly through the neatly trimmed yard of a narrow white clapboard little house with a gambrel roof, stopped at the garage, and looked carefully into Abby's backyard. She wished she'd changed her clothes. She felt as obvious as a nudist in her uniform. The house was silent. There was no sign of life. The window shades upstairs were drawn. The caller could have removed Abby, right after she called. But it would be dangerous to try and kidnap someone in a crowded neighborhood in the middle of the day. Of course it was also dangerous to stay in the victim's house. But most people weren't conscious of caller ID. And the caller would assume that holding a hostage would protect her. And maybe the caller thought it was the place so obvious that no one would look there. Or maybe the caller was stupid. Or desperate. Or maybe it was a hoax. Abby could be at work, entirely unaware. Molly should have called her office. But she didn't know where Abby worked, and there was no one to ask, and everything was moving too fast and here she was looking at Abby's backyard.

The house was built on a small slope so that it stood high on its foundation in the back. There was a door to the

cellar and a window on either side of the door. There was
no cover between her and the house. But it was only about
twenty feet. *There's no way to sneak,* Molly thought. *If
I'm the perp, I'm walking around the house looking out
windows, keeping an eye out for the cops. If I'm right, I
got three chances in four that she's looking out the wrong
window. I either make it or I don't. It's the best I can do.*
This was where normally you radioed for backup. Today
there was no backup. She took in as much air as she could
and blew it out and sprinted for the back of the house. No
one shot her. Nothing happened. She crouched against the
high foundation in relative safety. She was pretty sure she
couldn't be seen from the house.

Crawling to stay out of sight, she went past the cellar
window and tried the cellar door. Locked. She looked up
at the cellar window. The one on the left was locked; she
could see the latch. The one on the right had no latch.
She reached over and pushed up on one of the mullions.
The window didn't move. She took the flat end of the tire
iron and slipped it under the bottom of the window and
pried up. The window went up without much noise. Molly
dropped the tire iron and waited. No sound. No movement. She slid as close to the edge of the window as she
could and peered around it. There was a laundry room.
The laundry room door was closed. No one was in the
laundry room. Molly stood and boosted the window wide
open and climbed through. She stood in the laundry room
and listened. The house was quiet. But then she heard
footsteps on the floor above. She stood motionless. The
footsteps moved away. She strained to hear them and realized as she listened that she had been right. It sounded like
someone walking from one room to another, looking out
the windows.

Crouching next to the washer and dryer, Molly took off
her shoes and socks. It made her pants too long, and she
rolled the cuffs up over her calves. Then she straightened
and took out the gun. She'd never fired it at anyone. She
was a good shot on the range. She opened the laundry
room door. It was dimmer in the rest of the cellar. The cel-

lar stairs ran up from the front, the oil burner to the right. She could see the electrical board on the wall to her left. Barefooted and silent she went across the cellar and up the stairs. Policy was never to cock the piece until you were going to shoot. Standing on the top cellar stair, struggling to take in enough oxygen to keep up with her heart rate, Molly looked at the service pistol for a moment and then carefully pulled the hammer back. *Fuck policy!* She put her hand on the knob and listened again. She heard the footsteps get closer, moving slowly. Then they went past the door and faded into another room. Molly opened the door and stepped through in a crouch, the pistol aimed in the direction of the footsteps.

Bright. She was in a front hall. There were glass lights on either side of the front door, and sunshine streamed through the glass. Dust moats danced in the light. She saw no one. She stayed where she was frozen in her crouch, holding the gun with both hands, her finger on the trigger. *Not policy either.* Then she heard movement in the next room. She moved toward it silently, almost without volition, feeling nothing now, not even fear, her concentration so focused ahead of her that nothing else registered. In the living room, looking out the window, was a well-built blond woman in a black sweatsuit and white sneakers, carrying a black shoulder bag. Molly took two soundless barefoot steps into the room, and the woman became aware of her. She half turned, fumbling at her shoulder bag.

Molly said, "Freeze. Police." She stepped forward and got a handful of the woman's hair and pressed the muzzle of her service pistol into the woman's neck and slammed her against the wall face first.

"Don't move a fucking muscle," Molly said.

She hated how choked her voice sounded. The woman stayed where Molly had put her.

"What's your name?" Molly said.

"Faye."

"Okay, Faye. Let the purse slide off your shoulder."

Faye did as Molly told her and the purse fell to the floor. With her left foot Molly kicked it away.

"Now lace your hands behind your head," Molly said.

She moved the gun back enough so the woman could move her hands up. When the woman's fingers were laced, Molly got a good grip on the interlaced little fingers. Then she holstered her weapon, still cocked, and took her handcuffs off her belt and handcuffed Faye's hands behind her. Then she stepped away, took her service pistol out of the holster again. She didn't lower the hammer. She didn't know if Faye was alone.

"Where's Abby, Faye?" Molly said.

With her face still pressed against the wall, Faye answered, "Upstairs."

"She all right?" Molly said.

"Yes."

"Let's you and me go take a look, Faye. You first."

They went slowly up the stairs to where Abby was handcuffed to the bed. There were tears, Molly noticed, running down Faye's face.

chapter 6 5

Staying close to the edge of the road, unlit by streetlights
and undisturbed by traffic, Jesse felt as alone as he had
ever felt. More alone even than the day after Jenn moved
out. It was an alone of silence where there should have
been sound and emptiness where there should have been
activity. His jacket was warm enough for the sharp fall
night. He was comfortable, and if anything he was invigor-
ated by the slow swim ashore. Had he been walking alone
at night under the thin crescent moon for other purposes, he
would have felt buoyant. He didn't know where everyone
was. Hiding in their homes, he surmised. He didn't know
what had happened on the island. Robbery, he surmised.
But whatever had gone down before he got there, the
silence and emptiness excited him. He was full of energy,
and his legs felt loose and strong as he walked toward the
ocean side of the island where the restaurant was.

He heard the three shots before he could see the restaurant. He crouched beyond some trees and listened. Noth-

ing. Just the silence that followed the shots. He moved forward again slowly. The smell of the leaf mold under his feet was strong and mixed with the salt smell of the ocean. He could hear the water now, moving against the shore, and then he could see the restaurant in the dim light of the slim moon. There was no movement outside. The dim flicker of candle light showed through the windows. Near the back of the restaurant, there were no windows. Jesse dropped to his hands and knees and crawled carefully, staying in the shadows, toward the Dumpster. When he reached it, he squatted on his heels behind the Dumpster and looked. There were two shapes on the ground a few feet from him. He slid along on his belly now and reached the shapes. Two men. He felt them carefully. It was too dark in the shadows to see much. One with his throat cut. One shot more than once. That must have been the three shots. Nearby on the ground were two shotguns. Jesse felt in their pockets. Both men were carrying extra shotgun shells.

Okay, Jesse thought, *two less bad guys. More money for the ones that are left. Neither one is Macklin. Neither one looks like the Indian. I don't know the deal. I don't know who did the shooting, but now I know who got shot. I think they've got hostages. I don't know how many. I don't know how many bad guys there are. I can't go charging in there. I don't even know where exactly they are. Maybe they're not in there.*

Jesse scanned the shoreline in front of the restaurant and then the dark movement of the ocean. Close to shore, he thought he could make out the darker bulk of a boat. He looked hard and it blurred. He looked away and then let his eyes drift back, looking at it from an angle. The dark bulk was there.

Okay, now I know how they plan to get off. Doesn't do me much good. I can't do anything about it until I shake the hostages loose. Or even know who they've got or how many.

There was nothing to do at the moment, Jesse realized,

but what he was doing. Stay here in the shadows and
watch the candles glimmer in the windows and await
developments. He thought about Marcy and how afraid
she must be. He wondered how she was handling it. He
was scared himself, he knew, but he was used to it. He'd
been scared before, and he was able to put it away in one
corner of himself and proceed as if the rest of him were
not scared. Marcy had no experience with this kind of
scared.

Inside the restaurant, Macklin drank some of his martini
and smiled at Marcy.

"Okay, Marce," he said. "Let's get organized."

"Meaning?" Marcy said.

"Meaning you and the other ladies each take a duffel
bag and carry it out to the boat."

"Through the water?" Marcy said.

"Yep, it'll only be about three-and-a-half, four feet
deep. You hand the stuff up and then climb in the boat."

"You're going to take us?"

"A little farther," Macklin said. "We'll let you go next
stop."

Patty began to cry.

"I can't go. I have to go home," she said.

"Got to do what you got to do," Macklin said. "Get 'em
started, Crow."

Crow nodded and gestured at the women. All of them
were terrified to go. But they were more terrified of Crow.
Each took a duffel bag of pillage and started toward the
water, walking awkwardly in their high-heeled shoes.
Crow stood at the water's edge watching them. Freddie
Costa held his boat in as close as he could. Macklin stood
just outside the restaurant door, sipping the last of his
drink. Waist deep in the water Judy slipped and fell and
dropped her bag. Both woman and bag went under water.
Crow went in and caught the bag as it started to sink and
reached in with his other hand and yanked Judy up right.
He put the wet duffel bag back on her shoulder and shoved
her toward the boat. In deeper water, Pam floundered and

Crow salvaged her. Crow and the women reached the boat. Crow went up over the side of the boat as if he were on springs. The women handed in their bags and then went into the boat as Crow, one at a time, pulled them up by the wrists and over the railing.

Crouched in the shadows Jesse realized that the hostages were going. *I can't let them go.* It was less a thought than a feeling, an impulse, really, that seemed to originate in his solar plexus. *If I'm going to do it, I have to do it now.* The Indian was on the boat. Macklin was alone on shore. If he could take him out quietly . . . With his gun out, he ran silently from the shadows and along the side of the restaurant. He had to compromise silence and speed. If Crow looked in and saw him . . . The compromise failed. Macklin heard him, or sensed him, and spun toward him with his hand moving toward his gun.

"Freeze!" Jesse said, as hard as he could say it softly.

Macklin stopped and peered at him in the insufficient light.

"Goddamn," Macklin said. "It's you."

"Hands behind your head," Jesse said softly. "Fingers locked. Move."

Macklin grinned at him.

"It would have been a good move if you could have taken me out without a sound," Macklin said. "But now you're fucked."

Jesse knew Macklin was right. He held the gun steady on the middle of Macklin's mass.

"Maybe," Jesse said. "But I've got you, you son of a bitch."

"Or have I got you?" Macklin said, and raised his voice. "Crow," he yelled. "The police chief's here."

From the boat Crow said, "Yeah?"

Crow could only dimly make out the two figures in front of the restaurant.

"Shoot a hostage," Macklin said. "Get his attention."

"I hear a shot," Jesse yelled, "and Macklin dies."

"Do it," Macklin shouted.

On the boat, Crow said quietly to the women, "Climb over the side and wade ashore."

"What are you doing?" Costa said.

"I don't hide behind women," Crow said.

"But they're our passport out of here," Costa said. "They're Jimmy's passport."

"Get off the boat," Crow said.

The women scrambled over the side. Checkmated in front of the restaurant, Macklin and Jesse tried to see what was happening on the boat.

"Crow?" Macklin yelled.

On the boat, Marcy was the last woman over the side. As she hit the water, she heard Crow say to Costa, "Okay, crank it."

"What about Jimmy?"

"Jimmy's on his own. Get this thing out of here."

The big engines, which had been idling, roared to full throttle as the boat heeled away from the shore and headed for the open sea. The women stumbled and flailed and half swam in toward the shore. Neither Jesse nor Macklin moved out of the frozen tableau they formed in front of the restaurant door.

"That fucking Crow," Macklin said, staring out at the dark ocean.

"So," Jesse said, "I've got you."

Macklin looked back at Jesse.

"You might," Macklin said. "It looks like you might."

"Hands behind your head," Jesse said again, no longer speaking softly.

Marcy was the strongest of the women. She reached shore first and stood in the knee-deep surf helping the others ashore. Agnes Till was the last one. Except for Marcy, the women collapsed onto the rocky beach above the water line. When she got Agnes ashore, she turned and looked at the dark forms in front of the restaurant.

"Jesse?" she said.

"I'm here," he said. "Get on the ground and stay there until I tell you."

In front of the restaurant, Macklin began to back slowly away from Jesse.

"You know I fucked her?" Macklin said.

"That's your business," Jesse said, "and hers."

"Goddamned if Faye wasn't right," Macklin said.

He backed up a little more.

"Stand where you are," Jesse said. "I don't mind shooting you."

Macklin stopped.

"You could at least make it sort of a sporting thing," Macklin said.

"I'm not a sporting guy," Jesse said.

"You holster your piece," Macklin said. "We see who can draw and shoot quicker. Women can watch."

"Nope."

"Okay, just lower your piece. See if I can pull and shoot fast enough."

"Nope."

"You scared to play?"

"I don't need to play," Jesse said.

"That's all there is," Macklin said. "Take a chance, Jesse. See what you got."

Jesse shrugged.

"I won't tell you again," Jesse said. "Hands behind your head."

"I done time," Macklin said. "I ain't doing more."

"Your choice," Jesse said.

Macklin's hand dropped to his holster, and Jesse put two rounds into Macklin's chest.

Macklin went down slowly as if the strength were draining away in stages. Jesse went over and took the half-drawn gun from Macklin's hand and tossed it away. Macklin's breath was irregular and growing more so. He swallowed repeatedly. Jesse knelt beside him. Macklin muttered something that Jesse could not hear. Jesse bent closer.

"Faye," Macklin said. "I want Faye."

Jesse was aware of the women standing in a circle around him. Despite what he'd told them, they had walked silently up behind him and now stood staring down at the men. The smell of gunpowder still hung on the salt air.

Jesse felt the big artery in Macklin's neck. There was still a pulse, and then there wasn't.

chapter 66

Before she got into the big Coast Guard helicopter, Marcy Campbell put her arms around Jesse and held on to him as if there were a windstorm and he was a tree. Then she left him and got into the helicopter with the other women. They rose straight up and planed sideways and clattered over Paradise Harbor and landed on the high school football field, entering into an aurora of television lights and flashbulbs.

That was thirty-six hours ago and now having told everything she knew to Suitcase Simpson and the good-looking State Police SWAT team person, having been examined by a doctor, having showered and slept nearly eighteen hours, and showered again, and had some coffee, and orange juice, and eaten two soft boiled eggs and four slices of whole wheat toast with a butter substitute spray, she was waiting without much enthusiasm to do something she knew she had to do, without exactly understanding why she had to do it. She was sitting in a coffee shop in Government Center waiting to have lunch with Jenn Stone.

Marcy recognized her when she entered. She had made it a point to watch Jenn do the weather on Channel 3, and, while the forecast was laughable, she was as good-looking as Marcy had assumed. Several people recognized her as she came in, but if Jenn noticed she didn't let it show.

Marcy raised a hand as Jenn looked around the room, and Jenn saw her and came to the table.

"Hello," she said and put her hand out, "I'm Jenn."

"Marcy Campbell."

Jenn's grip was firm. Her body bespoke a personal trainer. Her hair was thick and intelligently cut. Her makeup was flawless. Her jewelry was quiet and expensive. The casual comfortable look of her clothes, Marcy knew, had cost her a lot of money. Jenn sat down opposite her, and Marcy knew she had taken the same inventory. And Marcy realized suddenly that Jenn looked a little like her. Younger. Probably better-looking, but Marcy could see that there was a resemblance. Jenn picked up the menu, a single mimeographed sheet of white paper.

"Have you ordered?"

"No, let's before we talk."

They were silent, briefly looking at the menu, and the waitress came and took their order. They both ordered a mixed green salad and a diet Coke, and they laughed at their common concern.

"It's a fight, isn't it?" Jenn said.

"You seem to be winning it," Marcy said.

Jenn smiled, comfortable with the compliment, accepting it as if it were expected.

The waitress reappeared with their salads and a bread basket.

"You wanted to talk about Jesse," Jenn said.

Marcy had thought about what to say since last night when she'd made her impulsive call. She had finally decided that she didn't know what to say and would wait and see what came out when the question was asked.

"Have you ever seen him at work?" was what came out.

"Marcy, he was a cop in Los Angeles when I married him."

"But did you ever see him being a cop, you understand?" Jenn got it quickly.

"You mean like you did?" Jenn said.

"Yes, and I know it's not my business, and I'm probably driven by gratitude and maybe post traumatic shock syndrome, but God if you had seen him."

"Tell me about it," Jenn said.

"He was, I don't know, there we were, like captives being led away, and then there was Jesse. One minute everything is hopeless and we're all terrified, and then . . ." Marcy couldn't think how to put it.

"Was he calm?" Jenn said.

"Yes."

"He would be," Jenn said. "And you saw him shoot this man."

"Yes."

"Was that awful?" Jenn said.

"No," Marcy said.

"Jesse can be very tough," Jenn said.

"And very brave."

Jenn nodded.

"Yes," she said, "very brave."

They both picked at their salads for a moment. The salads were mostly iceberg lettuce with a single red onion ring on it and two cherry tomatoes.

"This will not make us fat," Marcy said.

Jenn smiled.

"Nor happy," she said. She took a bite of salad. The dressing was on the side in a little cup. It was a bright orange.

"Sorry about the restaurant," Jenn said. "It's right near the station."

"That appears to be its only charm," Marcy said.

"I'll know better next time."

They each had a bite of salad.

"What is the point of you telling me about Jesse?" Jenn said.

"I guess I hoped it would help you make up your mind."

"He's told you about me."

"Yes."

"You lovers?"

"No, good friends."

"You fucking him?" Jenn said.

"Yes."

"But you don't love him."

"Been a long time," Marcy said, "since I thought those two were inseparable."

Jenn smiled without committing herself on sex and love. "And you like him a lot," she said.

"Yes."

"It's easy, isn't it," Jenn said, "to like him a lot. I like him a lot too."

"And love him?"

"Yes, absolutely, I love him," Jenn said.

"Then?"

" 'Then' . . . loving him and living with him are different things."

"I don't see why."

"You don't have to."

For the first time, Marcy heard the iron in Jenn's voice and realized that she was something a little more than a media cutie. It startled her a bit, though it didn't frighten her, and it made her feel better for Jesse, knowing he wasn't wildly in love with an airhead.

"No," Marcy said, "I don't. But it would be good if you did."

"I know some," Jenn said. "I know that Jesse loves me, but I know that he has to back off a little and give me some airspace."

"Obsessive?"

"Some."

"He doesn't seem obsessive to me," Marcy said.

"He's not in love with you," Jenn said.

"Ah-ha," Marcy said.

Jenn was quiet.

"If I could be a friend to both of you," Marcy said, "I'd like to be."

"Hard to figure how that will work," Jenn said.

"Might be worth a try," Marcy said.

"What's in it for you?"

"Payback, I suppose," Marcy said.

"What's in it for me?" Jenn said.

"A girlfriend isn't a bad thing," Marcy said.

Jenn finished her salad and broke off a piece of bread.

"May I call you?" Marcy said.

Jenn ate the piece of bread without butter.

When she had chewed and swallowed, Jenn said, "Will you tell Jesse?"

"No."

Jenn smiled at Marcy and nodded.

"Sure," she said. "Call me."

chapter 67

Jesse had Faye brought from her cell to his office. Molly stayed in the room.

"You can uncuff her, Molly."

Molly unlocked the cuffs.

"Sit," Jesse said.

Faye sat. Her face was without expression. Her eyes seemed empty. Jesse looked at some papers on his desk for a moment.

"Faye," he said. "We got you for assault and kidnapping."

Faye didn't say anything.

"You wanna explain to me what you were doing?" Jesse said.

Faye shook her head.

"Okay," Jesse said. "Then I'll explain it to you, and you tell me if I got anything wrong."

Faye was silent and motionless. Molly was equally still against the wall near the door, her service pistol looking, as it always did, a little too large for her.

"You're James Macklin's girlfriend."

"Was," Faye said with no inflection in her voice.

"And you saw me one night in the Gray Gull having a drink with Abby Taylor, and because of the way she was acting, you decided she must be my girlfriend."

Faye had no reaction.

"And when I came to ask you about Macklin and Cromartie, you knew that the thing on Stiles Island was already going down, and you got scared that I'd screw it up, so you went and grabbed Abby to use as a hostage. In case I had Macklin, you figured maybe you could barter my girlfriend for your boyfriend. You were wrong about me and Abby, but that wasn't your fault. You made a reasonable surmise."

Faye sat motionless, looking at nothing.

"Why'd you do that?" Jesse said.

Faye looked at him sharply. It was the first reaction he'd gotten.

"Why the fuck do you think?" she said.

"I figure it's because you loved him and would do anything you could to save him."

Faye was silent a long time. But she was looking at Jesse. Her eyes were alive. She began to nod her head slowly.

Finally she said, "Yes," her voice full of force.

Jesse leaned back in his swivel chair and rocked gently, balancing the chair with the tips of his toes.

"You got any money?" Jesse said after a time.

Faye didn't answer.

"She had a thousand dollars in her bra when I brought her in," Molly said.

Jesse nodded. Faye's face was pinched and white as if she were in pain.

"Go get her money," Jesse said to Molly.

Molly stared at him for a moment and then left the room without closing the door. Neither Faye nor Jesse spoke while she was gone. Molly came back into the room with an envelope and handed it to Faye.

"I'm going to take her for a ride," Jesse said.

"Alone?" Molly said.

"Yep."

"A female prisoner, Jesse? You're leaving yourself wide open."

"It'll be okay," Jesse said in just that calm way that Molly understood. It meant, *I will do this no matter what anybody says.*

Molly nodded once in submission and went back to the front desk. Jesse took Faye's arm, and they walked out to Jesse's official car and got in. Faye didn't say a word. She held the envelope that Molly had given her in her lap. She hadn't opened it. She didn't ask where they were going. Jesse went over the Tobin Bridge and turned off in City Square and drove back down past the Navy Yard to Faye's condo. When he got there and parked the car, he turned in the seat and looked at her.

"I know you don't believe it, but maybe you can remember that I said it. You will get over this. In time you will feel better. In time, and I know you don't want to now, you may meet another guy."

Faye shrugged, looking at the envelope in her lap.

"You're free to go," Jesse said.

Faye stared at him.

"I killed Jimmy because I had to," Jesse said. "I don't have to do anything to you."

Faye stared at him some more without moving.

"This doesn't wash it clean," Faye said.

"Nothing will," Jesse said. "In time it will be easier."

Faye still sat in the car, staring.

"Get going. Don't hang around here. Go far away, and I won't look for you."

Faye opened the car door and got out slowly and walked toward the stairs to her condo. Jesse waited as she went up. She took a key from the mailbox and opened her door. She stopped in the doorway and looked back at Jesse. Then she went in and closed the door, and Jesse backed the car around and drove back to Paradise.

When he walked into the station alone, Molly said, "Where's the woman?"

"She escaped," Jesse said and kept walking into his office and sat down at his desk.

Molly followed him in.

"Escaped?" Molly said.

Jesse nodded.

"The biggest collar I ever made," Molly said.

"You still get credit for the collar. I'm the one lost her."

"Lost her, bullshit," Molly said. "You let her go, you sentimental dumb son of a bitch."

"Molly, I am your chief."

"And you are also a sentimental dumb son of a bitch," Molly said.

Jesse shrugged. Molly came around the desk and bent over and kissed him on the mouth, then straightened and walked out of the office. Jesse got some Kleenex out of the bottom drawer and wiped his mouth.

chapter 68

It was Sunday morning. Jesse and Jenn were in Rowley, sitting at the counter of the Agawam diner, eating ham and scrambled eggs and home fries and toast.

"Do you know what happened to the ones that got away?"

"Not exactly. A big power boat washed up on the beach north of Port City couple days ago. There was a dead man in it. Guy named Fred Costa, had a record."

"How'd he die?" Jenn said.

The diner was warm with the smell of coffee and bacon. Outside the diner, along old Route One the trees were just beginning to turn.

"Bullet in the head."

"You think he was involved?"

"Maybe."

"And the Indian one?"

"Wilson Cromartie," Jesse said. "No sign."

"And all that money?"

"Gone."

"Still you got three of them," Jenn said.

"Actually, I got one of them," Jesse said. "They had already killed two of their own."

"And you saved the hostages."

"Sort of," Jesse said.

"What do you mean sort of?"

Jesse nodded at the thick woman behind the counter, and she poured more coffee into his cup. He added some cream, looked at it as it spiraled slowly into the coffee. He added two spoonfuls of sugar and stirred it, watching the color change. Then he took a sip.

"Well," he said. "Marcy Campbell told me that Cromartie let the women go."

"Really?"

"Yeah. He said he wasn't hiding behind women. If he'd held them and stayed put, I'd have been fucked."

"You think he was that gallant?"

"Gallant," Jesse said. "Nice word. I don't know. Maybe he just wanted all the money."

"He could still have taken them as hostages to protect himself until he got away."

"True," Jesse said. "On the other hand, he might have figured he could move better traveling lighter."

"I think he was gallant," Jenn said.

"If Fred Costa was the guy driving the boat, he gallantly shot him in the back of the head."

"You don't know that he was."

"No. Maybe we will. Fred was from Mattapoisett. State Cops are down there asking around, see if we can turn up anything. A connection to Macklin or Cromartie or either of the two dead guys."

"You've ID'd them? The other two men?"

Jesse smiled. A cop's wife, she fell into the jargon easily, and what sounded natural in the station sounded strange from her lips.

"Yeah, they've both done time. One's from Baltimore. One's from Atlanta."

"Well, I hope the Indian man gets away," Jenn said.

"Even though he seems to have abandoned his partner

to me and may have shot some guy to death on his boat and who knows who did the two guys on the island?"

"Yes."

"Because he was gallant about the women hostages?"

"Well, he was."

Jesse smiled at her.

"Okay," Jesse said. "And if I ever catch him, I'll tell him you said so."

"I hope you don't catch him. Is that Hopkins bitch still after you?"

"Probably," Jesse said. "But she's laying low at the moment."

"Be kind of hard to say you weren't doing your job right, with all the papers in the state calling you a hero."

"She'll wait," Jesse said. "I don't think she'll go away."

"She can't be happy you let me go."

"No."

"You let a woman go too," Jenn said. "Molly told me."

"She's supposed to keep her mouth shut," Jesse said.

"It's okay to tell me," Jenn said.

"You're special?"

"I certainly am," Jenn said.

"You certainly are," Jesse said.

Jenn was quiet while she sipped some coffee. Jesse ate some eggs.

"How you and short stuff doing?" Jesse said.

"Tony?"

"Yeah. He fall off his cowboy boots yet?"

"Oh, Tony's a news anchor, Jesse."

"So?"

"So he's frivolous."

"How about policemen, are they frivolous?"

"No," Jenn said.

Jesse bit the end off of a triangle of toast.

"So are you being frivolous with Tony these days?"

"I guess that isn't really your business, is it?"

Jesse felt the lump that was always there thicken again inside him.

"No," he said, "I guess it isn't."

Jenn patted his forearm. "I understand that it's hard not to ask," she said. "But sometimes the only way to keep something is to let it go."

"Divorce isn't letting go enough?"

"Maybe not," Jenn said.

"Well," Jesse said, "isn't that swell."

"Jesse, I'm not saying that this is the way it ought to be. But it is the way it is. I'm trying too."

"I know," Jesse said.

They were quiet while the counter woman cleared their plates. Jenn spent the time looking at his face.

"I'm very proud of you," Jenn said when the plates were cleared.

"Yeah," Jesse said. "I did all right."

"You did. And I'm proud of you for the way you're handling your drinking. And I'm proud of you the way you let that woman go. And I'm proud of the way you are staying steady on us. I know how hard it is."

"Like a rock," Jesse said wryly.

"And I love you," Jenn said.

"I love you too, Jenn. You know that."

"What was it that baseball person said about being over?"

"Yogi Berra," Jesse said. "It's not over till it's over."

"Well, he's right," Jenn said.

Jesse nodded. Jenn put her hand on top of his. Jesse felt slightly short of breath. He inhaled deeply.

What I need now, he thought, *is a drink.*

Robert B. Parker is the author of more than fifty books. He lived in Boston. Visit the author's website at www.robertbparker.net.

Look for the new hardcover from
New York Times bestselling author

The body in the trunk was just the beginning....

ROBERTBPARKER.NET

A MEMBER OF PENGUIN GROUP (USA) INC.

M565JV0410

Robert B. Parker

ROUGH WEATHER

Hired as a bodyguard for an exclusive society wedding, Spenser witnesses an unexpected crime: the kidnapping of the young bride, which opens the door for murder, family secrets, and the reappearance of an old nemesis.